Surgeon's Choice

RICHARD L. MABRY, MD

To all the authors who have given unselfishly to help this struggling writer on his road to writing. Thank you.

AUTHOR'S NOTES

As always, my thanks go to the women responsible for this novella getting "out there:" Virginia Smith, Dineen Miller, Barbara Scott, and Kay Mabry. Each one's contribution was essential, and I appreciate it.

Over a decade ago, when I set out to write a book about my struggles after the death of my first wife, I had no idea that God would lead me on this path of writing that thus far has included the publication of eleven novels and four novellas, as well as the non-fiction book I originally set out to craft. I'm amazed and a bit awe-struck. But, as always, *Soli Deo Gloria*—to God be the glory.

1

In the emergency room, Dr. Ben Merrick worked feverishly over the middle-aged Caucasian male. He glanced up briefly at the anesthesiologist. "Got him intubated yet?"

Dr. Rick Hinshaw answered from his position at the patient's head. "Just got the tube in and hooked him up to positive pressure." The rhythmic *chuff* of the machine pumping oxygenated air into the patient's lungs underscored the statement. "Now I'm about to put in a second IV with a large bore needle."

"Blood status?" Ben asked.

"A cross-match is going for six units," the head emergency room nurse said.

Dr. Carl Rosser, the ER doctor, looked at Ben. "What would you like to do until that's ready?"

Ben's gaze never strayed from the man on the gurney. "More O negative blood."

Dr. Rosser gave the order to a nurse. Then he took a penlight from the breast pocket of his white coat and shined it into the man's eyes. He ran his gloved fingers over the patient's bloody skull. "I'm pretty sure he has a depressed skull fracture, and it looks like his pupil's blown on that side."

Ben spared a moment to glance at the patient. "We need a neurosurgeon stat. See if you can get one here ASAP."

With a nod, another nurse turned from the group gathered around the gurney and headed for the phone.

Ben turned back to his work and put his stethoscope on the patient's abdomen, then percussed the area with his fingers. "He's most likely got free air under the diaphragm. I'll need a film to confirm it, but that can wait. A ruptured bowel is probably the least of his problems."

For maybe an hour, possibly more, the doctors and the nurses assisting them worked to save the man's life. But at last a sad look painted Ben's countenance. He shook his head and looked at the two other doctors gathered around the gurney—first at Rosser, then at Hinshaw. They grudgingly nodded their agreement with the decision everyone had worked so hard to prevent. "That's it," Ben said. "He's gone."

Ben's shirt was plastered to his body with sweat. He felt weak. He held out his hands and saw the fine tremor there, the effect of adrenaline pouring into his body. He took a deep breath and tried to shut down for a moment, but his mind wouldn't leave the problem. Had he done all he could? Was there something more?

And then, as he'd done countless nights in the months since Lawton Harrison died in the ER, Ben awoke suddenly from the nightmare. Sometimes he screamed, sometimes not. This time his dream ended in a silence that was somehow more terrible than any noise he could utter.

The sound of Ben slamming down the landline phone echoed through the surgeon's lounge of Freeman Memorial Hospital. He stooped to retrieve the papers that, until he hung up so forcefully, had been on the shelf beside the instrument.

Dr. Rick Hinshaw looked up from the copy of *Journal of Clinical Anesthesia* he was thumbing through. "Problem?"

"You might say so. I sort of did a favor for one of the hospital board members, so he thought he'd give me a heads-up."

"About what?"

"About the Harrison case. Since you were one of the treating doctors when he was brought into the ER, I guess you should hear this." Ben clenched his fists, wishing he had something to hit, or tear, or throw. "He says Dr. Kasner talked individually with several members of the hospital board this week and suggested that, based on the way I handled that situation, maybe it would be better if I were monitored in surgery for the next three months or so."

Rick put down the journal. "That's ridiculous. Why did he suggest that?"

"He said my actions showed inexperience, so he suggested a limitation on my practice. He wants a senior surgeon to review my cases and approve them before I schedule elective surgery. Kasner also thought it would be a good idea to have another surgeon scrub in during my operations for a while, sort of as a proctor."

"In other words, you could only do elective cases with someone looking over your shoulder. I don't know why he'd do such a thing."

"I've got an idea why, but it's only an idea." He took a deep breath. "Thankfully, the board didn't buy it, but my friend thought it would be a good idea to watch my step around Kasner. Have you gotten any flak over the Harrison case?"

"I've had a comment or two from a couple of surgeons, but I didn't let it bother me." Rich shook his head. "I wonder why Kasner is after you—or maybe us—for this."

"I think he's got it in for me, and you're caught up as collateral damage."

"Is everyone in the medical community here afraid of Dr. Kasner?" Rick leaned forward and rested his arms on his thighs. "Does he have something he holds over them?"

"I don't know. Maybe."

"If I were you, I'd steer clear of him. And I'll do the same." He started to pick up his journal, but let his hand hover in mid-air while he looked over at Ben. "Speaking of that case, have you heard anything more from the Harrison family?"

"Right after the incident, I talked with my malpractice insurance representative, who agreed that we did everything we could. Later I heard through the grapevine that Harrison's brother wanted to pursue a suit against those of us who were involved, but no lawyer would take the case."

Then the intercom came to life. "Dr. Hinshaw, we've brought up your next case. We're ready for you."

Rick stood. "I've got to go to work. Let me know if you hear more. And watch your back."

"Thanks." Ben took off his surgical head cover and ran his hand through his dark hair. "I sometimes wish I'd left the ER that night instead of turning to lend a hand when the call for help came."

Once more a tinny voice issued from the intercom. "Dr. Merrick?"

"Yeah, I'm here."

"We're ready for you in OR-2."

"Be right there." Ben stood.

I guess it's time to put this out of my mind and focus on my next patient. Still, I wonder if Kasner ... Well, never mind. We'll have to see what happens next.

Rachel Gardner grimaced, but tried not to let it show in her voice. She held her cell phone tightly as she paced the kitchen of her small house. "Mother, why won't you share what's supposed to be Ben's and my big day?"

"Dear, whether I'm there or not, you and Ben will still be married. But you should know that I have no intention of sitting next to your father, or for that matter even being in the same room with him—not for the wedding, not for the reception, never."

Rachel dropped into a kitchen chair and switched the phone to her other hand when she noticed how tight her grip had become. "I can't understand why you won't make this one exception for us."

"Yes, you do," Miriam Gardner said. "And Ben should as well. That is, if you've told him about what your father's done to our family."

For possibly the tenth time since she and Ben had gotten serious, Rachel wondered if she should have told her fiancé all about her father's past actions. But, although she had talked all around it, she hadn't given him the specifics. Instead, she'd introduced Ben to each of her parents separately, told him they'd been divorced for three or four years, and left it at that. She never found the right time to go into the details. He'd have to learn at some time, she supposed, but ... No, not now.

The conversation continued for another ten minutes, but her mother wouldn't budge. As far as Miriam Gardner was concerned, if Bill Gardner would be there, she wouldn't. Rachel ended the call with a hollow feeling.

She'd had a tough day in her position as a nurse on Two North, and this talk with her mother hadn't helped the fatigue—both physical and mental—that she felt. Rachel was still sitting in the kitchen chair holding her phone when it rang. When she saw it was Ben calling, she smiled for the first time since she got home.

"How was your day?" he asked, as he always did.

"I imagine it was about like yours," Rachel replied. "Would you mind coming by for a few minutes so we can talk?"

"I've got to make rounds at the hospital, but I can come over after that." He hesitated. "Is everything okay?"

Her hesitation was brief, and she hoped Ben hadn't noticed. "Everything is fine. I just have something about the wedding to discuss with you, and I'd rather do it face to face. Is that all right?"

"Sure."

Rachel sighed. She'd fill him in when he got there—about her mother, but probably not about her father.

Ben experienced a pleasant feeling of anticipation when he parked his car in front of Rachel's house. As he strode up the walk, he could already picture her meeting him at the door—her petite build and stature placing her lovely face well below his own six foot-plus height, her blue eyes sparkling as though she knew a secret she wasn't ready to share, her brown hair hanging loose around her face, freed from the ponytail she usually wore at work. He could hardly believe this beautiful woman was in love with him and in a few short weeks would be his wife. He tried to focus on her and put his other worries out of his mind.

Rachel answered the door and immediately pulled him into a long hug, followed by a kiss that was more passionate than usual. She finally stepped away. "Thanks for coming over."

"Never a problem," he said. "I like the greeting, but when

I talked with you on the phone, I sensed something might be wrong. What's up?"

"Let's sit down and I'll tell you." They settled on their usual place—the living room sofa. "When you called, I'd just finished talking with my mother."

"And?"

"She's still not coming. She knows that you and I are planning the wedding and paying for it. All I want is for her and Dad to be there—him to walk me down the aisle, her to fuss over me and beam a bit as her only daughter gets married. But she's adamant."

"Anything I can do to change her mind?"

"No, not really. I needed to share that, I guess." She looked at him. "Was this a bad day for you?"

Ben hadn't intended to burden Rachel with his frustration over Dr. Kasner's actions, but decided she'd better know about it. After all, they had said they'd always be honest with each other. "I got a call from one of the members of the hospital board." He went on to explain what had happened. "I guess Kasner is out to get me."

"And this time he's using the Harrison case?"

"Rick Hinshaw was in the ER and helped that night too. He said he'd gotten a little professional pushback, and Kasner might be behind it as well. But it doesn't seem to worry Rick."

Rachel shook her head in apparent disbelief. "Are you going to do anything about this?"

"What can I do? Just practice the best medicine I know how," he said. "Although if I'd known it would cause me this much trouble, I might have thought twice about going against Kasner when that lawyer asked for an opinion on his actions."

Rachel got up and walked around behind him. She put her hands on his shoulders, snuggled her head next to his, and whispered in his ear. "If you hadn't stepped up to the plate, I would have thought less of you. Someone had to stand up to him, and I'm glad it was you. When you opposed Dr. Kasner, you made an enemy, but you gained my admiration."

He turned his head to look at her. "Then it was worth it."

Ben sipped from the cup of coffee in front of him and watched the front door of the deli. He had been planning his Saturday activities when Bill Gardner called to ask if they could meet here. When Ben asked why, Gardner had said, "I'll tell you when I see you."

He'd only met his future father-in-law a couple of times, but he was sure he'd recognize him from the commercials Gardner did for his auto dealership. The ads on local TV and newspapers showed the man as a symphony in black and white: black suit, white shirt, silver tie, all setting off a pleasant face topped by hair that was jet-black except for a touch of gray at the temples.

Ben really didn't know much about either Bill or Miriam Gardner except that they'd divorced after Rachel left for nursing school. When Ben asked for details, Rachel acted as though she were too embarrassed to talk about them. She'd say, "My parents are divorced. My father ... well, what he did was bad, and my mother is still angry about it. But I promise you that neither of them will be a part of our life together." Obviously, Bill Gardner had done something that Rachel didn't want to talk about. She'd tell him when she was ready.

When Gardner walked in, he went right to Ben's table and took a chair. "I appreciate your meeting me here."

The man was nervous. Ben didn't think it was only from meeting his daughter's fiancé again. No, there was something else causing him to act—what was the word? Jittery.

"Mr. Gardner, would you like some coffee? Perhaps a pastry?" Ben asked.

"It's Bill. And no thank you. Let me get this over with."

"Okay."

It took a minute, but eventually, Gardner got it out. "I need some money."

So that was what this was about. Ben figured the auto dealership was doing okay, but perhaps there was some sort of short-term need for a small amount of money. "I'll do what I can to help, but realize that I'm still paying off my student loans and trying to get my surgical practice going, so I don't have much in the way of resources. How much do you need?"

The deep breath and exhalation that followed told Ben he wasn't about to like the response. He didn't.

"About forty thousand … no, make it forty-five thousand dollars."

Ben wasn't sure he'd heard correctly, so he asked Bill to repeat the figure.

"I need forty-five thousand dollars. And the sooner the better."

Now it was Ben's turn to inhale deeply, then let out his breath through pursed lips. "Bill, maybe some doctors have lots of money, but I'm not one of them. I thought maybe you needed a couple of hundred dollars for some reason, but that much money is way beyond me. If you were talking about getting it from a bank and wanted me to co-sign a note, I doubt they'd find me a decent guarantor."

"No, I don't want to borrow from a bank. I was afraid you couldn't help me, but I thought I'd ask." Bill stood. "Thanks anyway. I'll handle it."

"I'm really sorry I couldn't help, and I hope you understand. Why do you need the money?"

Gardner shook his head. "Never mind. Forget I asked."

Obviously, Rachel's father wasn't ready to give him any details about why he needed the money. Ben decided to switch the conversation to something pleasant. "Rachel and I are looking forward to seeing you at the wedding. I presume you'll still be there."

Bill replied in a hoarse voice. "Sure. But I need to work this out first." Then he turned and walked out.

Ben was still sitting in the deli when his phone rang. It was the hospital, with a patient in the emergency room he needed to see. He put down his coffee cup, paid the cashier, and pushed open the door. Then he stopped when he saw his car parked at the curb with two flat tires. A valve stem lay on the sidewalk next to each rear tire. He screwed in the valve stems, then searched in his trunk for the pressurized can he carried for such emergencies—one that would temporarily air the tires until he could make it to a service station.

At one time, Ben would have classed this as random mischief by neighborhood children. Now he wasn't so sure. Was it an act of revenge from the brother of the man in the ER he couldn't save? Had Kasner arranged this as yet more harassment? Or had Bill Gardner not wanted to be followed? What next?

2

At noon on Saturday, Rachel rummaged through her cupboard, making her shopping list, when she stopped to answer her phone. Ben.

"Hey," she said. "Have you had lots of calls this morning?"

"Only a couple of medical situations, and I handled them over the phone," he said. "But I had a meeting this morning I need to tell you about."

"You make it sound serious."

"It may be. Your father called me earlier this morning and wanted to get together. We met at the deli where you and I get coffee sometimes."

Rachel had tried to keep Ben's contact with her father to a minimum. The rational part of her brain told her his past wouldn't affect Ben's love for her, but her family didn't lend itself to rational thinking sometimes. She wished it were different, but that's the way it was. "What did he want?"

"He wanted money."

"I wonder why. How much did he need? A hundred dollars, a couple of hundred?"

"How about forty-five thousand dollars?"

Why was her father trying to get that much money together? Had he dug himself into another financial hole? She sighed inwardly. Her mother had warned her. Rachel had made her way into the living room while she talked. She lowered herself into a chair there, still holding her cell phone. "Are you sure he asked for that much?"

"Yes. He asked for forty-five thousand dollars."

"Did he say why he needed it?"

"I tried to find out, but when I told him I couldn't help him with that much, he ended the conversation and left," Ben said.

"Hmm. I wonder …"

"Wonder what?"

"Nothing." Rachel bit her bottom lip when she thought of the reason her parents divorced. Had he reverted to his old problem again? If so, that would explain why he needed that much money, although the amount astounded her. Her father had promised both her and her mother that he'd conquered his drug habit, but maybe he'd broken that promise. "Look, Ben. Why don't you let me handle this? I'll check into it and see what I can find out."

"I can do it," Ben said.

"No, this is my family. I know the people to call, the doors to peek through without causing a stir. After I know more, I'll tell you." She paused. "Thanks for letting me handle this. I know it's sort of second nature for you to take over, but—"

"Can you hang on a second? I've got another call coming in."

"You go ahead. I'll get back to you later."

Rachel continued to sit there, the dead phone in her lap, her mind churning. She searched for another reason her father needed money. Maybe he wanted it for some type of medical procedure. No, that couldn't be it. His dealership provided good insurance for everyone who worked there, and she was certain he was covered.

Was the money for her mother? No, she wouldn't go to her ex-husband for help, no matter what. Besides, her mother had money of her own, didn't she? The most obvious reason kept popping up in Rachel's brain, but when it did, she shoved it down as deep as possible.

Don't think the worst. Although right now she couldn't think of any other reason why her father needed that much money unless he was hooked on drugs again.

Well, she'd find out the truth—even if it hurt. She picked up her cell and began dialing.

Ben's call was from the emergency room at Freeman Memorial Hospital. He recognized the voice on the other end of the conversation.

"Ben, this is Carl Rosser in the ER. I understand you're on general surgery call this weekend. I have a young man with low-grade fever, elevated white count with a left shift, but not much tenderness in the right lower quadrant. I don't want to miss a case of appendicitis. Want to come in and have a look at him?"

"Sure, Carl. I'll be there in about fifteen or twenty minutes."

As Ben climbed into his car, he wondered about Carl. The case might call for a second opinion, but there were times when Carl's mind seemed elsewhere. He acted less sure of himself than Ben would expect of an ER doctor. He'd need to watch Rosser more closely.

He was halfway to the hospital when a large SUV pulled out of a side street, straight into his path. Ben simultaneously hit the brakes and swerved, narrowly avoiding a collision with his smaller Subaru Legacy. Even though he missed the other vehicle, he ran over the curb and slammed into the stop sign pole. Then the right front side of his car slowly sank as the tire deflated.

By the time Ben exited his car, the SUV was nowhere to be seen. He looked around for witnesses, but the street was empty. Of course, this could have been a normal fender-bender, but could it represent a change of heart by one of Harrison's relatives, an attempt at retribution? Or might Kasner be behind this as well? Certainly, he wouldn't go this far—or would he?

Ben called the ER and talked to a nurse on duty about his crash. "I'll be there as soon as I can."

"I'll give Dr. Patel the message," she said.

"Wait a minute. I thought Dr. Rosser was on duty."

"He had to leave for a bit," she replied. "We're pretty slow, and I think he had an errand to run."

Ben was still pondering this when he opened the trunk of his car and took out the jack.

Rachel usually was off on weekends, but when Ben was on call she traded so she could work some of those days, especially Sundays. She figured she was more likely to see him if she was caring for patients on Two North than if she was in her usual place at church, or sitting at home. They might even have a chance to grab a sandwich together at noon in the food court.

That was why Rachel was on Two North that Sunday morning, standing outside the door of a patient's room, when she heard Ben's voice behind her.

"Got a minute?"

At the nursing school Rachel attended, the rule was stressed: No PDA—public display of affection. She turned and whispered, "I wish we could slip into the utility room and close the door. That way I could give you a hug and kiss."

"I'll take a rain check." Ben smiled and briefly caressed her shoulder before looking around to make certain no one was watching.

"Is your car okay?" Rachel asked.

"I changed the tire and put on the spare. Then I used a tire iron to straighten the fender skirt on the right front. It doesn't look pretty, but it's drivable," Ben said. "But how about your phone calls. Find out what's the story with your dad?"

"I made a couple of calls yesterday and gave the people who would know every opportunity to tell me, but they said nothing. I thought about calling my father and confronting him, but I think I'll leave that for last." Rachel looked at her watch. "I've got to get back to work. Are you making rounds?"

"Yep, I did an endoscopic appendectomy yesterday afternoon. I'll probably discharge him—"

Both looked up as they heard the overhead PA system announce, "Code Blue, Two North. Code Blue, Two North."

"That's this wing," Ben said.

"And there's the room." Rachel pointed down the hall to where a call light flashed above the door.

"I'd better see if I can help out." Ben turned and hurried toward 201— the room in question. It was a private room, opposite the nurses' station. The man inside was post-operative patient John Pence. Rachel hurried after Ben, but by the time she reached the open door, she could see two doctors and as many nurses already gathered around the bedside. She wasn't needed, but it was hard to turn away. She stepped back, but continued to watch from the doorway.

Ben was on the right side of the bed. "Got that board under his mattress?" A nurse opposite him indicated it was securely in place, and he nodded. He placed his hands on the patient's breastbone, one on top of the other, and started CPR. He repeated the maneuver rhythmically and rapidly.

Quietly, Rachel started humming the BeeGee's song, *Staying Alive*, a cadence for resuscitation she'd first learned during a CPR class.

She stepped aside as another nurse wheeled a crash cart into the room, stopping at the bedside, and quickly plugged in the thick electrical cord. "Defibrillator is ready if you need it, doctor."

Ben looked at the monitor at the head of the bed. "Looks like asystole, not v-fib, but thanks."

As curious as she was, Rachel needed to get back to her duties caring for the other patients on the floor.

At the nurses' station, Sheila Britton spoke to Rachel as she passed by. "Cardiac arrest, right?"

Rachel nodded. "When I walked away, they were doing CPR. The monitor showed total asystole." Cessation of a heartbeat was treated with drugs, including the injection of adrenaline directly into the heart, followed by cardiac massage. The treatment was standard, but it didn't always work.

Sheila shook her head. "Poor man. His heart simply gave out, I guess. I suppose it couldn't stand the emergency surgery Dr. Kasner performed the other day."

"What was the procedure?"

"Strangulated inguinal hernia," Sheila said.

"Think he'll make it?"

"The man's eighty-five years old and has a history of severe coronary artery disease." Sheila looked around to make certain she was alone with Rachel. "The cardiologist who saw Pence suggested a local anesthetic and a quick operation. Instead, Dr. Kasner operated under general anesthesia, and he took over two hours. I think it was too much for the man's heart."

As though to bear out the nurse's words, Ben slowly walked out of the room and turned toward the nurses' station.

His downcast eyes, slumped shoulders, and defeated expression told her all she needed to know.

Ben knocked on the door of Rachel's home on Sunday evening. After she opened the door for him, she stepped into his arms and pulled his head down for a kiss. Then, with her arms still around him, she buried her head on his shoulder. When they separated, he asked, "Still thinking about the man who died earlier today?"

She nodded. "I think all the nurses were pulling for Mr. Pence to make it, and when he didn't … Anyway … thanks for helping out today." Rachel led him into the living room where they settled onto the sofa.

"Anyone would have done the same," Ben said. "What did Dr. Kasner have to say when the head nurse notified him?"

"He told her he'd call the oldest son, who was listed as next of kin, and tell him that his father had a heart attack and died. He'll sign the death certificate tomorrow."

"That's it?" Ben tried without success to keep the emotion out of his voice. "He wasn't coming to the hospital? He didn't offer to meet with the family? Sounds like he didn't much care that one of his patients died."

"I get the impression from listening to Sheila talk that Dr. Kasner doesn't exactly take a personal interest in his cases anymore. Honestly, I think he's coasting toward retirement."

"How long's he been practicing here?" Ben asked. "Twenty-five years, thirty maybe? I guess it's possible he's always been that way, but if that's the case, why is he considered the dean of surgeons here in Freeman?"

"Would you have answered that Code Blue if you'd known the patient was one of Dr. Kasner's?"

"Sure. I meant it when I said that anyone would have done what I did. Of course, this is simply another occasion for Kasner to find something wrong with my actions." He thought for a moment. "I think I might call my malpractice carrier tomorrow and tell them about the incident."

"Do you need to do that?"

"I don't think I did anything wrong, or—for that matter—anything that Kasner can twist and use against me. But I'd rather be safe than sorry."

Rachel reached out and took his hands. "That's enough about Dr. Kasner."

"You're right," Ben said. "Did you find out anything more about why your father needs money?"

Rachel shook her head. "No, when I got home I decided not to make any calls. Tonight, I want to relax and forget all about my family and the hospital and everything else." She leaned back. "I intended to make something for us, but—"

"Never mind." Ben pulled out his cell phone. "Want Chinese or pizza?"

Ben had a restless night on Sunday, and as a result he rolled out of bed early and arrived at his office before his receptionist or nurse. He pulled his key from his pocket, but found the door already open. When he went inside, the waiting room was total chaos—seat cushions slashed, a coffee table overturned, a fichus plant taken from its container and thrown against the wall, scattering potting soil.

He steeled himself against what he'd find when he walked into the treatment rooms, but it was still difficult to view such senseless destruction. Instruments scattered helter-skelter, bandage material strewn on the floor. The glass doors of the treatment cabinets were askew, and vials of local anesthetic on the shelves were smashed. Surprisingly enough, his office suffered the least. A few file drawers hung open, his chair was overturned behind the desk, but that could all be put right in a short while.

He was still standing in his office, surveying the damage, when he was joined by Earline Bullis, his receptionist, and Betty Wilson, his nurse. Earline, a young African-American woman, had come to him straight out of business school and was a gem. Betty was an older woman, a widow, who had quickly caught on to his routine. On more than one occasion, Ben reflected that he'd be lost without these two women.

"I should be able to clean up the treatment rooms in a couple of hours," Betty said. "Those glass doors will need to be replaced, but we can still function."

"And I'll call our insurance carrier and see about replacing those slashed chairs," Earline said. "As I recall, we've got a fairly light schedule today. I'll move some patients around."

Betty patted Ben's shoulder. "Do you want to call the police and report this, or shall I?"

Ben returned his desk chair to its normal position and sat down. "I will. This isn't the first incident. I guess it's time for me to report them all."

Rachel pulled out her cell phone in the Two North nurses' lounge on Monday and prepared to make a call, but it rang before she could punch in the first number. Since the call came from Ben, she smiled when she answered.

"I was about to phone my dad," she said. "But I'm glad for a chance to put it off. What's up?"

"There was a break-in at my office overnight," Ben said. "I thought you should know about it."

Her heart sank, knowing how much time, energy, and money Ben had put into his offices. "Who would do such a thing?"

"I have a few ideas."

"Did they steal any drugs?"

She listened as Ben related what he found when he came in that morning. When he finished, she said, "Are you going to discuss the other incidents with the police?"

"I've called it in, and when someone comes to take my statement, I'll mention them, but I doubt they'll take it seriously. In the meantime, I suppose I'll need to be careful."

Rachel gripped her phone tightly, frowning. "Ben, it won't do you any good just to be careful. You'd better be prepared to defend yourself if this escalates. Didn't you tell me you have a pistol?"

"I have a nice little five-shot revolver that I bought right after I went into practice. But I decided that guns can be more dangerous than being held at gunpoint, so it's safely in the drawer of my entryway table."

"I'd feel better if you started carrying it."

"But I wouldn't," Ben said. "Look, I've got to go. I wanted you to know about this latest episode, but please don't blow it out of proportion. It's probably just another break-in to a doctor's office." There were muffled voices in the background. "I've got to go. Love you."

"Love you too." Rachel decided there was nothing she could do right now about Ben's safety except pray, and she was doing enough of that already. Meanwhile, she had a call of her own to make before her break period was over. With a sigh, she tapped in the number for her father's cell phone.

Her father was truly addicted to his smart phone. In fact, he gave out his phone number in every one of his TV commercials. His philosophy was that having someone you could call day or night was important to his business. His cell was never farther than an arm's length away, which is why Rachel frowned in puzzlement when it rang six times, then rolled over to voicemail. She couldn't recall the last time she'd called him, and he didn't answer.

Maybe he's on another call. No, that would be even more unusual. When her father saw another call was coming in, he wrapped up his conversation, promising to call that party back if needed, so he could get to the next one. How many times had she heard him say it? "I don't like keeping people hanging on. If they call to ask a question, I'll answer it. If they want an extended conversation, let 'em come in to the dealership and I'll talk face to face."

Rachel's time was running out. Since she'd gone this far, she might as well try one more number. This one rang only once before it was answered with a cheery, "Gardner Motors."

She didn't recognize the voice, but then again, receptionists seemed to come and go at the dealership. Rachel wished her father had a private line into his office, but he'd always said that his cell phone was enough. "Let the sales reps handle those other calls."

"This is Rachel Gardner ... Mr. Gardner's daughter. Is he around?"

The answer came without hesitancy. "No, I haven't seen him all day. But Mr. Durbin is here. Maybe he can help you."

Rachel was left hanging before she could respond. In a couple of minutes, a familiar voice answered. "Rachel? This is Joe Durbin."

"Joe, have you seen my dad?"

"Nope. And he doesn't answer his cell. Of course, he was supposed to see some bigwigs from the factory, and he may be tied up with them."

Dad didn't answer his cell. That's somewhere between unlikely and impossible. She looked at her watch. Her next call should be to her father's home phone, but she didn't have time. And she'd have to leave her own phone in her locker until she got off work. Rachel sighed. "I've got to go, Joe. When you see Dad, tell him I'll call him at home tonight."

As she stowed her cell phone and closed her locker door, Rachel was anything but relieved by the results of this last call. Now she was more worried than ever about her father. Then, there was Ben. The incidents in his life seemed to be escalating. Who was behind them? And what was next?

"So, can anything be done about this?" Ben spoke to the policeman who sat across from his desk, writing in his notebook.

The gray hair at the officer's temples and the stripes on his sleeve led Ben to place his age at nearly fifty. *I wonder why he's taking calls like this one?* The policeman looked up at Ben. "Honestly—probably not."

"But—"

"Look at it this way," the policeman said. "Someone deflated your tires. Common mischief. We see it all the time, especially since school's out for the summer. You had a fender-bender. Happens every day, and usually the larger vehicles—like an SUV—don't suffer as much damage as a smaller car like your Legacy, so when there are no witnesses, they don't stick around."

"What about the break-in here?" Ben waved his hand at his trashed office.

"C'mon, Doc. We have a drug problem here in town. A couple of detectives have been looking into it for months. In this case, an addict broke into a doctor's office, searching for drugs in your treatment rooms. When he didn't find any, he took what he considered to be revenge."

"Will you at least check for fingerprints?" Ben asked.

"Why? This is a doctor's office. We'll find your prints, those of your staff, and probably a couple of dozen people who've been through here—patients, cleaning people, pharmaceutical reps Think anything significant will turn up?"

Ben opened his mouth, but closed it without saying anything. In his mind, he considered another possibility. But there was no hard evidence—only his suspicions.

"Let us know if anything more happens, Doc." The officer closed his notebook. "Your secretary can get a copy of my report to send to the insurance company."

And all I can do is keep my eyes open and hope this doesn't escalate.

3

A

s he walked out of his office on Monday evening, Ben wanted nothing more than to go home, ignore the phone, and pull the covers over his head—to shut out the world. But he needed to talk with Rachel to tell her what the policeman said. Besides, he was curious about her progress with her father, so he pulled out his phone and called her. "Hey, I called it a day and thought I'd check in with you."

"Actually, I was about to call you. Could you come over? It would help if we could talk about this face-to-face."

"Sure, I'll be there shortly," Ben said. "Have you eaten? Want to go out for something? Order something in?"

"I doubt I'll be able to eat, but I can put together a sandwich for you."

"What happened when you called your dad?"

"We'll talk about it when you get here," she said.

Ben thought about Rachel as he drove to her home, but decided it was fruitless to guess the outcome of her phone calls. She had probably found out more about her parents, and it was unlikely to be good.

Rachel met him at the door. Her hug was no less enthusiastic, her kiss no less passionate, but Ben could tell something was bothering her. "Want to tell me about it?"

"In a minute." Rachel turned toward the kitchen. "You can listen while I make you a sandwich."

"I'm not really hungry either."

"Ben, let me make you a sandwich. I'll feel better if I'm doing something." She motioned him to a chair at the kitchen table. "Anything more about the break-in at your office?"

"Not really. The police don't think much of the series of incidents." He related the details of his time with the sergeant. Rachel seemed distracted as she listened, so Ben moved on. "Now what did you find out about your father?"

"I tried to call my dad's cell phone this afternoon. He always answers—night or day. I've never known a time over the past several years when he didn't keep it handy. But this time there was no response."

"Maybe the battery ran down."

Rachel was shaking her head before he finished. "No. He charges it every night as it sits on the nightstand. Anyway, then I called the dealership, but they hadn't seen him. I ended up talking with Joe Durbin."

"Who?"

"The general manager. Joe's been with Dad since they started the dealership. I guess that he's Dad's second in command." She pulled out bread and laid two slices on a plate. Then she shook her head and took two more. "I probably should eat something too," she murmured, more to herself than to Ben.

"What about Joe what's-his-name?"

"Joe hadn't seen Dad all morning. He thought some guys from the factory were supposed to be with my father today."

"So maybe he's ignoring the phone because of them."

Rachel shook her head. "I can't believe he'd ignore the phone, even under those circumstances. And my name would show on the Caller ID. I'm pretty certain he'd take my call, regardless of who was there."

"Did you try his home?"

Rachel added lunch meat and cheese to the bread. "Mayo or mustard?"

"Either one." Ben asked again. "Did you try to call your father's home?"

"There was no answer. Dad has a little apartment where he's lived since he and Mom divorced. It's small enough that he can get to his landline from any room before it rolls over to voicemail." She put the sandwiches together and cut each in half.

"So, he hasn't answered his cell, which is unusual, and you can't reach him at home. The town where he lives is only fifteen minutes away. Why don't we go check on him?"

Rachel shook her head. "He's a grown man, and he's only been out of contact for a day or so." She put the sandwiches on plates and added chips before placing them on the table. "There's not enough for a missing person report. You know though, given his age and that he lives alone, maybe the police could do a welfare check."

"Sounds like a good idea." Ben bit into his sandwich.

She chewed her thumbnail. "No. Something may have happened to his cell phone. Let's not panic … yet. Maybe he'll show up at the dealership tomorrow morning, get the message, and call me."

"And if he doesn't, I can check on him after work tomorrow afternoon. Would you like that?"

"Yes." She sat down and picked up a half of her sandwich. "Knowing you're in this with me helps."

Ben's cell phone rang at ten that night. He had already changed into the scrub suit that he, like many other doctors, favored instead of pajamas. He checked the Caller ID—Dr. Art McNabb, an anesthesia specialist with whom he sometimes worked when Rick Hinshaw wasn't available.

"Art, this is Ben. What's up?"

"I'm sorry to call so late, but I've been tied up on an emergency case until now. Earlier this evening I talked with the woman you have scheduled for surgery in the morning. She doesn't have any cardiac findings, but her history made me a bit suspicious, so I ordered a stat EKG. It looks okay, but I wanted to touch base with you."

Ben couldn't recall why Art McNabb would be calling about a case, and—for that matter—why he talked like he would be doing the anesthetic for it. Then he remembered. Rick Hinshaw told him this morning he had an obligation that would take him away from the hospital on Tuesday, and Art would be stepping in.

"Ben, did you hear me?"

"Sorry, I was thinking of something. Sure. If you're happy with her status, let's go ahead with the case. But thanks for letting me know."

As Ben ended the call and picked up the journal he'd been using to put him to sleep for the past few nights, he wondered what Rick was doing that would take him away from his duties. As far as Ben knew, the anesthesiologist, who was single, lived a life that consisted of work, eat, sleep, repeat. Honestly, Ben had never considered that Rick had a life outside of medicine. He'd have to see if he could find out when his colleague returned to work.

Rachel climbed into her bed that night with a sense of unease. She reached to her nightstand and picked up the book she'd been reading, but replaced it unopened. Instead, she tried to organize her thoughts, but they kept running into each other.

She still didn't know why her father had called Ben, needing so much money, although she feared he'd slid back into his drug habit. Oh, there were other explanations, but all she could think of were the bad ones. Suppose he'd gotten into debt to his drug supplier? What if the men who'd come to collect left him unconscious or even dead?

Of course, death would put an end to everything, while her father's continued drug use—the monster in her closet that she'd tried to ignore—might wreak havoc for years. She could picture a cycle of rehab stints, then a brief period when he was clean, followed by a recurrence of the problem. It would certainly cost money, either to support the habit or go into rehab, which would explain his request to Ben. Even if he was still clean, his drug habit would always be there, waiting to ruin his life and the lives of everyone he loved.

Rachel reached past her book on the nightstand and took up the well-worn Bible that lay beside it. She opened it randomly and turned to the Psalms, taking comfort—as she always did—from the words there. "He who dwells in the shelter of the Most High will abide in the shadow of the Almighty. I will say to the Lord, 'My refuge and my fortress, my God, in whom I trust!'"

Ben's surgical case went well on Tuesday, and Art McNabb's handling of the anesthetic was flawless. He asked Art casually if Rick had mentioned why he planned to be gone today, but the other doctor had no idea. Ben shrugged. "I guess we'll find out soon enough."

He spent the afternoon in his office seeing patients, signing papers, and fielding phone messages. Ben kept waiting for the call from Rachel, the one that would tell him, "Everything's okay with Dad. He called me as soon as he found out I was trying to talk with him. And you'll really laugh when you hear what he wanted that money for." But the call never came.

Several times Ben thought about calling Rachel, but he didn't—sometimes because he was interrupted, sometimes because he thought about it and decided not to bother her. She'd call when she knew something.

Finally, when he'd seen his last patient and finished with the papers on his desk, he decided that since his fiancé had finished her shift a couple of hours ago she should have talked to her father by now. He had a feeling the results weren't good, or he would have heard from her before this.

Ben dialed Rachel's cell number, and she answered after a single ring. "Hi, Hon. Got a minute to talk?" he asked.

"Sure. I was just about to call you."

He tried to ease the tension he felt creeping up in his neck. "Have you been able to get in touch with your father?"

There was a catch in Rachel's voice. "No. I tried his cell, his home, and the dealership, and there's still no sign of him." She caught a quick breath that was almost a sob. "So, I finally decided to call mother. And there's no answer from her either."

"I've got to go by the hospital and see my post-op patient from this morning. Then I'll drive over to Carlyle and check on him. I don't think I've ever been to his apartment, so I'll need to get that address from you."

"I can do better than that," she said. "I'm going with you."

Rachel watched the houses and fields go by as Ben drove the short distance from Freeman to Carlyle. She wondered once more why her mother wouldn't put aside the enmity she held against her ex-husband long enough to see their only child get married. Of course, this also reminded her that, just as her mother or father rarely drove fifteen minutes to see her, she didn't visit them very often. She vowed to remedy that.

When she had been unable to contact her father, Rachel had a brief hope that perhaps her folks had reconciled. Maybe they'd remarried in a brief ceremony and were away for a few days, taking a second honeymoon and not wanting to be disturbed. Rachel shook her head, realizing that this was the sort of dream a child of divorced parents might have. It wasn't likely. For now, she'd settle for finding out why her father had stopped answering his phone.

Ben reached over and squeezed her hand. "Worrying won't help, Sweetheart. We'll find out soon enough. And I'm here with you. Meanwhile, don't drive yourself crazy writing scenarios that might fit the circumstances."

Rachel was silent for a bit. Should she tell Ben what she'd done last night, and each time she or a loved one was facing a crisis? Ben wouldn't pooh-pooh her, of course. He was a believer like her, but he simply wasn't inclined to turn problems over to the Lord. He was a surgeon, and his philosophy was that he wouldn't think of calling on God unless he was unable or unlikely to handle a problem himself. She hoped that one day he'd think differently, but today was not the right time or circumstances to discuss it.

"Okay, we're almost to the Carlyle city limits. Where do we go from here?"

Rachel snapped out of her reverie and gave Ben directions. It only took five minutes to reach the apartment complex where her father had lived since the divorce. She'd been there a couple of times, but Rachel realized her last visit was more than four months ago. If things worked out … No, she'd deal with the situation as it unfolded. Promising she'd visit her father was too much like trying to strike a bargain with God.

"Want to stay in the car?" Ben asked.

Rachel was already unfastening her seat belt. "No, he's my father. I'm going with you."

Bill Gardner's apartment was on the ground floor. There were two newspapers on the tiny porch, and the place was dark and silent when Ben looked through the glass panes in the door. There was no answer to either his ringing of the doorbell or his repeated knocking.

"I guess he's not here," Rachel said. "Maybe I should find the superintendent or someone who can unlock the door."

Ben worked his way around the bushes that guarded the front windows. He peered into the living room between his cupped hands. "Nothing in the … Wait. I can see the open door to the bedroom." He looked for an instant more before pulling out his cell phone. "I don't think we should waste time finding someone to unlock the door. I'm calling the police."

4

When the police arrived, Ben looked at his watch. Less than ten minutes had elapsed between his call and the patrol car pulling up next to theirs. That wasn't long in ordinary circumstances, but it seemed like an eternity to him—mainly, because he'd seen an unmoving pair of legs jutting from a doorway inside the apartment.

"Why didn't you break down the door?" Rachel asked. "Or maybe break out a window and climb through? Why are we out here waiting?"

The easy explanation would have been that the person inside was probably already dead. And that person was undoubtedly Rachel's father, but until there was firm identification he didn't want to tell her that. "I thought this was the best way to go." He pointed to the officers emerging from the patrol car. "Let's let them handle this."

Two policemen climbed from the car, put on their hats, and slowly approached Ben and Rachel. He noted that, although there was no overt threat visible, they kept their right hands close to their holstered pistols. One, the car's driver, was a middle-aged man with sergeant's stripes on the sleeve of his short-sleeved uniform shirt. The other was a young blonde woman. She deferred to the older man, but despite her youth, she'd already acquired the slight swagger Ben had observed in most police officers.

The male officer spoke first. "I'm Sergeant Carver. What seems to be the trouble?"

Ben looked at Rachel, but she shook her head.

Okay. I guess it's up to me. "I'm Dr. Ben Merrick and this is my fiancé, Rachel Gardner. We live in Freeman. Miss Gardner has tried without success for a couple of days to contact her father, so we drove over here. No one answered the door, but when I looked through the window, I thought I saw a man's legs sticking out of the doorway of the bedroom."

"So, we don't know if he's alive or dead." Seeing Rachel flinch, the sergeant said, "Sorry."

"There's no movement," Ben said. "If there were, I'd have broken down the door myself."

Sergeant Carver nodded. "But there's still a possibility the person inside is unconscious."

Ben realized the policeman was establishing a reason for forcing entry. "Right."

The hinges of the front door were on the inside, which meant it swung inward. He put his hand on Rachel's shoulder and gently guided her a few steps away. "We'll let the police get inside."

When there was no response to Carver's repeated pounding on the door and his cries of "Police," the two patrolmen checked to make sure Ben and Rachel were clear of the door. Then the sergeant took a stance on the lock side, while his partner moved to the other side, each slightly away from the door itself. Both drew their weapons. After a glance at the other patrol officer, Carver raised his foot and brought it forward so the heel struck above the lock. It took three kicks before the wood splintered and the door swung inward.

Both officers scrambled into the apartment. They separated and in a few seconds declared the small living space clear except for the bedroom, which they left for last. Ben and Rachel followed at a safe distance. As soon as he reached the point in the living room where he had a full view of the legs sticking out of the bedroom, Ben turned to Rachel and grasped her shoulders. "Don't look."

Ben had only met his future father-in-law two or three times, but he had no doubt about the identity of the man lying on the floor—Bill Gardner. He wore the pants to one of the dark suits that were his trademark. The collar of his white shirt was loose, and his black tie had been used as a tourniquet. It now lay beneath his left arm like a symbol of mourning.

The sergeant knelt and felt for a pulse, but Ben was certain he wouldn't find one. If his clinical experience wasn't enough to tell him Gardner was dead, the needle and syringe still protruding from the corpse's bare left arm was definitely a clue, not only to his status, but also to his mode of death.

Although Ben had never actually seen someone who had died of a drug overdose, he expected their expression would be one of anticipation, waiting for the "rush" of whatever drug they were injecting. In this case, Bill Gardner's eyes were frozen in a stare, his mouth wide open in a silent scream. The pathologist would undoubtedly tell the police more, but to Ben, there was something wrong here.

Rachel didn't have to be a nurse to know her father was dead. Books said dead people appeared to be asleep, but that wasn't true. They looked dead. As a nurse, Rachel had seen dead people before, and there was no doubt that her father was no longer alive. She stood back, alternately wiping tears from her eyes and wondering what she could have done differently. Could she have saved him if she'd acted sooner?

When the coroner's van arrived, Sergeant Carver led her and Ben into the kitchen. Ben pulled her into an embrace, and she wept on his shoulder. She heard the gurney enter the apartment and roll into the bedroom. Having seen it before, she visualized her father's body being lifted into a black bag. She heard the zipper close, ripping out her heart. Ben pressed her head against him, probably hoping to spare her the sight.

What seemed like a couple of hundred questions followed, most of them aimed at Rachel, even though Ben tried to deflect as many as possible. Finally, the sergeant said, "I think that's enough for now." He looked at his notebook. "I have your contact information in case we need to know more. You're free to go."

Rachel took a shuddering breath. "What … What about notifying my mother? I know they're divorced, but still—"

"We can do it either way. If you'd like someone from the department—"

Rachel wiped away her tears. "No, I'll do it. I don't know how she'll take it, but it would be best coming from me." She took another deep breath and blew it out. "And what about … the arrangements?"

"The medical examiner will contact either you or your mother when he's finished with … when he's finished. You can call me after you've talked with her, and I'll relay the message." He fished out a card and handed it to her. "We'll take care of getting things locked up here." He touched her shoulder. "I'm sorry for your loss."

"Thank you." Rachel stuck the card in the pocket of her slacks. She looked out the window at the van carrying her father's body away. Then she turned to Ben. "I don't guess there's anything more for me here."

"No," Ben said, rubbing her arm. "I think we need to go to your mother's home. Do you want me to break the news to her?"

"No, I'll do it. But I'll be glad to have you with me."

She and Ben arrived at Miriam Gardner's house in less than ten minutes. Rachel wished it had taken longer. Actually, she didn't want to do this at all, but there was no getting around it. Nevertheless, this was the hardest thing she could ever remember doing.

Rachel stood on the porch and took several deep breaths before she turned to Ben, who was reaching for the doorbell. "You should knock. The bell doesn't always work."

He nodded. "Ready?"

She turned away for a moment and closed her eyes. *God, give me the right words to say.* Rachel swallowed a couple of times, squared her shoulders, and said, "Yes." She wasn't really ready. But she was as ready as she'd ever be. Maybe her mother wouldn't be home. Maybe she wouldn't answer the door. Anything to postpone this awful moment.

Ben rapped on the door, and the sound reverberated inside. Rachel turned to look at the front yard. The grass was neatly mowed. The flowers in the beds had been recently watered, and there was not a weed in sight.

She recalled that one of the things her mother insisted on during the divorce proceedings was staying in the house where her daughter had grown up. Miriam Gardner certainly hadn't let the house deteriorate. If anything, she'd maintained it like … like a monument. Rachel didn't know if that was in honor of her, or her mother's way of telling Bill Gardner, "Look what you let slip away."

"I hear footsteps," Ben said.

The words Rachel had carefully crafted for breaking the news to her mother flew from her mind. She had no idea now what she should say.

The door opened and Miriam Gardner stood there, smiling. "What a pleasant surprise." She was an elegant woman who looked at least five years younger than her real age. Even when she had been going through difficult times holding her marriage together, Rachel's mother had hidden from Rachel and the rest of the world any outward evidence of the turmoil in her home. And now that the divorce was long past, she continued to be an active, vibrant woman. Her only concession to the pain she'd experienced in the past was her continued refusal to associate with her former husband.

Her mother stepped forward to embrace her daughter, and then she looked over Rachel's shoulder. "Ben, it's good to see you too." Her mother's brow furrowed. "What's wrong? Come in and tell me about it."

Rachel struggled to keep her composure. "Mom, I wish I didn't have to bring you such bad news."

Her mother stared at her with apparent alarm. "What is it, dear?"

Rachel opened her mouth, but the words wouldn't come out. Instead, she started to cry. She felt Ben's arm around her shoulders, and heard him say, "Mrs. Gardner, I'm sorry to tell you that the police discovered the body of Rachel's dad—your ex-husband—a couple of hours ago."

"Where? How?"

"At his apartment," Ben said. "He was dead when we got there. And they found a needle still in his arm. It appears he overdosed."

Either her mother was genuinely saddened by her ex-husband's death or she was a great actress. Rachel watched as tears formed in the woman's eyes. She shook her head, turned without a word, and walked slowly from the entryway hall into the living room, where she lowered herself onto the sofa.

Ben took a chair near the sofa where Rachel and her mother sat talking in low tones interspersed with periods of silence. A couple of times he started to say something, but decided it was best to let the two women have their private moment of grief. Finally, both women rose. Miriam dried her eyes with the tissues her daughter supplied, nodded once, and walked slowly from the room.

Ben rose and walked over to Rachel. He hugged her, and she put her head on his shoulder. "Care to fill me in?"

"She's pretty broken up about this. I think there's a lot of 'it could have been different,' and 'Why couldn't he leave the drugs alone?'"

"They must have loved each other once," Ben said softly.

"I think so, although even before I left for college, I could see him pulling away. Mom had adjusted to the divorce, but now she's left to clean up the mess Dad left behind."

He nodded his understanding. "What about notifying other family members of his death?"

"Dad's parents are dead, and he had no siblings. And I'm sure the police will be talking to the people at his car dealership," Rachel said. "So, I guess once Mom and I know about it, that's about it. His friends and acquaintances will learn soon enough."

"Will you be in charge of arranging his services?"

"Mom wants to take care of it, and I suppose she knew him better than I did. She wants me to call Sergeant Carver and ask him to have the Medical Examiner's office notify her when they release his body."

"Do you want to stay with her?" Ben wondered whether he should cancel the surgery he had scheduled for the morning.

"I asked her about that, but she said no. She has several friends she's close to —a couple of divorcees and one or two widows—and she'll probably call them. They're part of her church group."

Miriam walked into the room. Her eyes were dry, but red, and her expression showed the grief she felt. She hugged her daughter, then him.

"I appreciate your letting me know, Rachel. I'll call you sometime tomorrow."

Ben's fiancé and her mother hugged each other again, and then he and Rachel walked to his car. They rode toward Freeman in silence for several minutes, Rachel staring out the window, before he spoke up. "The police may have more questions for you. I'm pretty sure they'll want to find out where your father got his drugs."

"I have Sergeant Carver's card. I'll stay in touch with him. So far as I'm concerned, the flow of information works both ways. I want to know everything the police find out." She continued to stare out the window. "I have a hard time believing Dad was back on drugs. He promised me …"

Ben started to respond, but decided to remain silent. For him, the question wasn't whether Bill Gardner died of an overdose. The evidence was pretty clear. He was certain that detectives already were looking to answer the question of who gave him the substance that ended his life. The toxicology report would tell them what the substance was. Their next question, of course, would be the identity of the person who gave it to him.

Wearing goggles, a surgical mask, and head covering, his clothes covered by a blue paper gown, Dr. Jim Carpenter looked ready to perform an operation. In a manner of speaking, he was, but there was no anesthetist at the head of the table. The patient lay perfectly still, even when Carpenter's scalpel made a large Y-shaped incision through the pale flesh.

"I was supposed to be off today," he muttered. He reached for the bone saw he'd use to open the chest cavity.

Carpenter's presence in the county morgue was the result of a case of the flu severe enough to confine one of his fellow pathologists to bed. That set off a chain reaction that ended with him standing over the body of William Gardner. He continued to mumble about the detectives involved in the case. "'Put a rush on the autopsy.' 'Can't wait until tomorrow.' 'Let the Chief Medical Examiner do the post-mortem.' So here I am, Mr. Gardner. What have you got to tell me?"

The pathologist grumbled throughout the procedure, but that didn't mean he took shortcuts. As usual, he did a thorough post-mortem examination. One of the reasons he liked forensic pathology was that each of these cases was a puzzle, and the clues he gleaned from the autopsies were often enough to not only pin down a cause of death but point the police toward a murderer.

Dr. Carpenter had noticed when the body had been brought in that the needle and syringe were also presented for his inspection. The offending instruments had been dusted with black powder, so they had already been checked for fingerprints. He also studied the crime scene photos.

The pathologist had seen dozens, maybe hundreds, of people who overdosed on drugs. This was obviously death due to a self-administered substance, but the expression on the corpse's face caught and held his attention. Carpenter knew the police were working hard to roll up the ring that supplied the drugs. He wanted to document his findings, but even more, he kept his eyes open for clues that might further the investigation.

When he had finished the exam, he looked up at the morgue assistant, who—either wisely or through boredom—remained silent during the entire procedure. "Close up the incisions, would you? And then we can let the funeral director—whoever the Gardner family has chosen—we'll let them take over from here."

As he was about to leave the room, he paused. "Be certain those vials go today for toxicology exams. Matter of fact, put a rush on them."

"Anything unusual about this one?"

"Call it pathologist's intuition," Carpenter said. "All the standards, especially opioids, of course. But also assay for fentanyl, and if they can do it, carfentanil."

"Sure, but why?"

"I don't have anything that proves it except the expression on the man's face." He tossed his mask, head covering, and gloves into the container by the door. "When the substance started flowing into his veins, I think he realized he was injecting more than heroin. It's likely that what this man OD'd on was a drug called Gray Death."

Ben yawned behind his mask during his case Wednesday morning. He was grateful that as a surgeon—especially one who trained at Parkland Hospital—he was used to operating after little or no sleep. That was certainly his status today. And he'd started his case about a half hour late at that, which meant the nursing staff was less than happy about the situation.

Fortunately, he had only one patient on the surgery

schedule this morning, a middle-aged female with chronic gall bladder problems. He had done this operation—endoscopic cholecystectomy—so often during his residency training that he had jokingly said he could do it in his sleep. However, he had no intention of sleeping on the job right now—not only because the patient deserved his best efforts, but because Dr. Kasner seemed to have his spies everywhere, waiting to report any failing on Ben's part.

Later, as he exited the recovery room, the cell phone in the pocket of his white coat vibrated. He wasn't due in the office for another couple of hours, but something may have come up. When he looked at caller ID, though, he saw the call wasn't from his office. Rather, it was from the police.

"Dr. Merrick."

"Doctor, this is Detective Bradford of the Freeman Police Department."

Ben frowned. Initially, he'd thought this was some sort of routine follow-up to his report of the break-in at his office. But would a detective call about that? "How can I help you?"

"I wonder if you could come down to the station sometime today? The sooner, the better."

"Why?" Ben asked.

"We'll tell you all about it when we see you. What time can you be here?"

Ben looked at his watch. He had almost two hours before he was due in the office, and his curiosity would keep him on tenterhooks until he found out why the detectives wanted to talk with him. "I'll come right away."

"Ask for me or my partner, Detective Amy Wilson. Unless we're out of the building for some reason, we'll try to see you as soon as you get here."

Ben drove to the police station and parked in a space marked "Visitors." The inside of the building looked nothing like what he'd seen on TV, but he recognized the hive of activity. The desk sergeant directed him to a bench and said the detectives would see him soon.

"Soon" turned out to be twenty minutes. Forced to wait, Ben watched police officers, some in uniform and others in civilian clothes but all with that "police" look, come through the front door. Some of them, usually the ones who were alone, greeted the man behind the desk. Others, walking in groups of two or three, concentrated on their conversations without even glancing at the desk. At no time did Ben see anyone in handcuffs or even gripped by a hand on the biceps. Maybe there wasn't a lot of crime in Freeman. But more likely, the criminals were brought in through another door.

He was about to look at his watch for probably the tenth time when a bass voice said, "Dr. Merrick?"

He looked up and saw a large, African-American man standing in front of him. He wore a gray suit, a blue shirt with a button-down collar, and a patterned red tie. "I'm Charles Bradford. I appreciate your coming over. I hope we won't keep you long."

In a moment, Ben was seated in what he figured was an interview room. He took the chair on one side of the table. On the opposite side, Bradford sat down and held up a hand. "My partner will be here shortly." He busied himself with papers he carried with him. In a few moments a younger, Caucasian woman entered and took the chair next to Bradford. "This is Detective Amy Wilson."

If Bradford was ebony, Wilson was ivory. They were polar opposites in many ways, not just the color of their skin. Ben estimated the male detective stood almost a head taller than six feet. Wilson probably topped out at a few inches over five.

Bradford's suit most likely had been purchased off-the-rack from a mid-range store, Wilson's tailored, dark-blue pants suit looked expensive.

After Bradford made sure Ben didn't want anything to drink, the detective asked permission to record the interview. When he agreed, Bradford punched a button on the recorder, tested it, and said a few words to identify the people present. Ben noted the detective included the information that he was giving a "voluntary statement."

Ben frowned. Statement? Did he need a lawyer?

"Dr. Merrick, were you acquainted with Dr. Rick Hinshaw?"

When Ben heard his colleague referred to in the past tense, a chill passed through him. Something was wrong. And he was pretty certain he was about to find out.

5

Ben had one more patient to see on Wednesday afternoon before he could duck out of the office. He was anxious to talk with Rachel and tell her about his discussion with the two detectives earlier in the day. But he figured his news would keep until he saw her in person. In the meantime, he'd have a look at Mrs. Brown.

Phyllis Brown was a fifty-four-year-old housewife who, according to her chart, was seeking a second opinion about breast surgery. Her records had been sent over from the office of the other surgeon she'd seen, but Ben preferred to start fresh and reach his own conclusion without any possibility of prejudging the situation. He'd read the other doctor's notes afterward.

Ben knocked briskly on the exam room door and entered. "Good afternoon, Mrs. Brown. I'm Dr. Merrick. I understand your insurance company requires a second opinion before your scheduled breast surgery. Tell me about it."

"I told your receptionist that my insurance company requires this," the patient said, "I'm not sure whether they do or not. Actually, my visit is more for my peace of mind."

Ben wondered what was coming next, but maintained his professional demeanor. "Suppose you tell me what's going on, and I'll give you my best advice."

The history he got was of a woman who was careful to do breast self-examination every month, as well as getting a mammogram annually. She did this because it was a recommended procedure, but especially since her mother and grandmother both had fibrocystic disease. "With that history, I wanted to get ahead of things."

"And you felt a mass."

"That's right. I waited a week and it was still there, so I asked my family doctor for a referral to a specialist. The one I saw agreed there was a nodule, so he recommended removal of the mass—a lumpectomy, he called it—with either chemotherapy or radiation if it was positive."

"Did he order a mammogram, or suggest any other tests before he operated?"

"I asked about that." Mrs. Brown shook her head. "He said they weren't necessary. He'd seen enough patients with stories like mine that he didn't think he needed anything more."

Ben hurried to erase the frown that flitted across his face. "Tell you what. Let me have my nurse get you ready, and I'll examine you. Then we can talk."

While Betty helped Mrs. Brown, Ben reached for the phone on his desk. But about the time he started to dial Rachel's number, his secretary Earline tapped on his office door. "Dr. Merrick, the ER is on the line. Can you talk with them?"

"Sure." It turned out to be a relatively simple question, but by the time he'd dealt with it, his nurse signaled from the open doorway that Mrs. Brown was ready.

His exam was straightforward. The woman had a small cystic mass in the lower outer quadrant of her right breast. There were no nodes in the area, and the skin over the cyst was intact without redness or tenderness. He felt no other masses in either breast. Mrs. Brown had brought a chest X-ray, which appeared clear to Ben (although he wasn't certain why one was done).

"I'll let you get dressed, then Betty will show you to my office. I think it should be simple to deal with this mass."

"Without surgery? But that's what the other doctor thought was necessary." Her eyes reflected her anxiety.

Ben took the chart Betty handed him, but didn't look at it. He decided to relieve some of Mrs. Brown's concerns. "If I'd seen you initially, I'd have begun by congratulating you on performing regular self-exams. A mammogram would be helpful, and I'd probably order one because there might be another mass hiding in there. Assuming the mammogram only showed this one, and since you have a family history of fibrocystic disease, I'd want to see if this was the same thing."

"How would you do that without surgery?"

"I'd numb up the area and use a fine needle to aspirate—to suck out—the fluid if I could. If the aspiration yielded fluid, that probably would be the end of it, since these cysts are benign. However, if for some reason I suspected tumor cells might be hiding in there, I could send the material for what we call a cytology exam.

"If I was unsuccessful at attempts to do an aspiration, I could use an ultrasound scan to determine if the mass was cystic. Of course, if the mass were solid, it would need to come out, as the other surgeon suggested. Otherwise, I'd suggest continued regular self-examinations, along with annual mammograms—and we'd help convince your insurance company of that need."

Mrs. Brown heaved a sigh that Ben was sure could be heard throughout the office suite. "Will you take care of me for this?"

"I don't like to take patients away from other doctors," he said. Then he looked at the chart that had arrived by

FAX earlier that day. The doctor she'd originally seen was Dr. Herbert Kasner.

"It's your choice," he said. "I'd suggest you talk with your husband. If you still want me to take over, I will. In the meantime, don't worry about it."

Rachel had gathered her dirty clothes and was sorting them when her phone rang. Glad of anything that let her postpone her washing, she smiled when she saw the call was from Ben.

After the usual greetings, he said, "Why don't I come by for you and take you to RJ's for a quiet dinner? We can talk there."

"Ben, I'm wearing a bleach-spotted pair of jeans, a tee shirt that's too big, and sneakers with holes in them."

"And you probably look great." Ben chuckled. "I'll give you thirty minutes to change if you insist. Then I'll swoop down on you in my magic carriage with the crumpled fender and carry you away."

Then he hung up. Rachel shrugged and decided that a nice dinner out was better than the left-overs she'd planned to reheat, so she left her laundry on the floor and hurried to get ready.

True to his word, Ben rang her doorbell half an hour later. He met all her questions with the same answer. "Later."

At the restaurant, Ben asked the hostess if they could sit at a back booth, the one with the most privacy. The waitress arrived to take their drink orders—sweet tea for Ben, the unsweetened variety for Rachel. When they were finally alone, Rachel said, "Enough stalling, Ben. Tell me what's up."

"No, you first." Ben leaned across and spoke to Rachel in a soft voice. "Is there anything new with your father's death."

"I called and left a message for Sergeant Carver that mother wanted to be in charge of Dad's ... body. She's already picked a funeral director. The service will be at her church, and the two of us will help put together the memorial service for him."

"Good. And your mother? How's she doing? We can visit her tonight if you'd like." Ben took her hand.

"She's all right. I called her after I left the message for the sergeant, and I offered to come over. We talked for quite a while, but she told me there was no need. She has her friends and church group for support. I'll see her this weekend sometime."

Ben started to say something, but she stopped him. "I think we should change the subject. Did you want to tell me something ... something important?"

Ben took deep breath, then blew it out through pursed lips. "It started with Rick Hinshaw. You know he administers the anesthetic for most of my cases."

Rachel reached for her water glass and took a sip. "Yes. What about Rick?"

"He got another doctor to fill in for him today. He said he had to take care of some personal business."

She frowned. "And the importance of that?"

"Rick had an appointment with the local detectives, but he didn't show up. Detective Bradford—that's the man with whom I met— told me how Rick tried to impress on him the importance of getting the interview as quickly as possible. He had an appointment with Bradford for 8:00 a.m., but he didn't show. He'd been so insistent that when the detective hadn't heard from Rick by noon he sent a patrol car by his apartment. They found him dead of a gunshot wound to the head."

Rachel covered her mouth with her fist as she inhaled. "That's terrible. And they wanted to talk with you because you were a colleague and friend?"

Ben shook his head. "It started out that way. But by the time it was all over, Bradford and his partner Detective Wilson had given me a Miranda warning and let me know that I was among the list of suspects for Rick's killing."

Rachel shook her head. "Why would they do that?"

"When Rick set up his meeting with the detectives, he said he had information about the drug ring that's been in operation in this region for a while. He was pretty sure a doctor—maybe more than one—was involved. Bradford theorizes that whoever shot Rick did so to keep him from telling what he'd learned."

"And—"

"And the police are questioning Rick's circle of colleagues. Since I was probably closest to him, they've got me at the top of the list."

He leaned back from the table as their salads were served. When the waitress had left, Ben shoved his plate aside. "I think I need a lawyer. Matter of fact, I probably should have had one with me when I went to the police station."

Ben tried to put Rick Hinshaw's death and the police investigation out of his mind as he worked on Thursday. When his colleagues mentioned Rick's passing, he tried to act surprised at the news. Ben figured that whatever the police wanted people to know would soon become common knowledge, and other than that he'd keep mum. But throughout his morning surgeries—the anesthesia done by Art McNabb—Ben tried to think of an attorney he could engage to represent him. But he kept coming up empty.

As he entered the surgeon's dressing room, he was almost hit by the opening door. He stepped away and Dr. Kasner, an elderly, overweight man dressed in scrubs, waddled through, his eyes fixed on the chart he held. Kasner pushed his glasses up on his nose with a stubby finger and looked at Ben. When he recognized the younger surgeon, his countenance was that of a man encountering a bad smell.

"I didn't realize you had a case on the schedule this morning, Dr. Merrick," Kasner said.

"Actually, I operate fairly frequently. You'll be happy to learn that my practice is taking off." He considered saying more, but decided that was enough.

"Well, I suppose I'll see you again then."

He said it with a sneer, and Ben thought what he really meant was, "Are you still here?" This was the first time Ben had seen Dr. Kasner up close in a while. The man's appearance certainly didn't inspire confidence, nor did his manner. Ben determined he needed to redouble his efforts to avoid Kasner, even though they worked in the same specialty at the same hospital.

Ben changed clothes and headed for the physicians' parking lot, trying to decide whether to pick up something to eat before heading to the office, when his cell phone rang. He looked at the caller ID and smiled. Rachel. "Hey, this is a pleasant surprise."

"I wanted to call you, even though I only have a short break."

"Too short to meet you in the food court?"

"Sorry," she said. "I asked one of the nurses to bring me a sandwich in return for my staying on the floor. I wanted to call you instead of taking lunch."

"I love hearing your voice." He smiled. "I can hardly wait until we're married, so I get to hear it more often." *Assuming I'm not in jail by that time.*

"Actually, I called for a reason. I remembered one of my classmates in nursing school talking about her brother, who was getting his criminal law practice started. Unless you've come up with the name of another attorney."

"I haven't," Ben said.

"I found a Christmas card from her after I got home last night. I called and asked if her brother was still in practice, and she said yes. Let me give you his name. You can do some research and see if he'd be a good lawyer for you to engage."

"With the Internet, I can get a fair amount of information on him. I hope he's both good and local," Ben said. "I'll let you know this afternoon."

He pulled a pad out of the glove compartment of his car and jotted down the name Rachel gave him. Maybe this guy would work out. He hoped so.

6

Ben called Rachel's cell on Thursday afternoon. "Are you headed home from work?"

"Yes. Do you have some news for me?"

"I looked up the name you gave me—Robert MacArthur—in Martindale-Hubbell."

"What's that?" Rachel asked.

"It's a directory of attorneys, with evaluations by their peers and their clients. Not only is this man rated highly, but his practice is right here in Freeman. I called him, and I'm on my way to meet him now."

"What about … Oh, this is Thursday afternoon, so you're off. Do you want me to join you there?"

"Sure. It will save me telling you about it this evening."

"Give me the address. I'll meet you there in fifteen minutes."

The law offices of Robert MacArthur and Associates were, as one might expect, near the court house. Ben was getting out of his car when Rachel drove up. He glanced around carefully to make sure it was safe before he took Rachel's arm and helped her from her car.

Rachel's concern for him showed in her expression. She had a wedding coming up soon, her father had taken his own life with an IV overdose, and yet her thoughts centered on

Ben. Sometimes he wished he could be more like her—less self-absorbed.

"Try not to worry because I'm consulting an attorney, Rachel. I'm probably being overly cautious, but I'd rather have representation now than bring in someone later and have to update them."

She squeezed his arm. "Remember, I'm in this with you all the way."

Ben nodded and pushed open the door of the building. They found the office easily. The black-and-gilt letters on the upper glass portion of the door read, "Robert MacArthur and Associates. Attorneys at Law." Once inside they both looked around the small, nicely appointed waiting room they'd entered. Six leather-upholstered chairs, a couple of coffee tables with current magazines, two ficus plants, and a reception desk manned by a young blonde straight from the Donna Karen catalog—a standard, high-end waiting room, suitable for an attorney, accountant, or almost any other white-collar enterprise.

They had no sooner checked in with the receptionist than one of the two doors behind her opened and a forty-something man emerged, smiling at them. He had ginger-red hair, cut fashionably short and receding to a pronounced widow's peak. He wore the pants to a charcoal-gray, pin-striped suit, a white shirt with a spread collar, and a quiet blue tie. Dark-blue suspenders and black wing-tip shoes completed the outfit. Ben almost laughed. If someone had asked central casting to send over an attorney, this man would have come knocking. All he needed was a briefcase, and Ben felt sure he had one of those in his office—probably more than one.

The man stretched out his hand. "I'm Bob MacArthur."

Ben shook his hand. "Dr. Ben Merrick." He inclined his head toward Rachel. "And this is my fiancé, Rachel Gardner."

"Miss Gardner, if you'd like to make yourself comfortable here—"

"If it's okay with you, I'd rather Rachel hear it all," Ben said. "I have no secrets from her."

MacArthur considered this. "For now, that's fine with me. If the situation changes, we'll deal with it." He ushered them down a short hall and into what appeared to be his office. After they were seated—MacArthur in a swivel chair behind a mahogany desk and them in padded client chairs across from him—the lawyer pulled a legal pad toward him. "Okay, tell me about it." He fixed Ben with a steely gaze and added, "But realize that you haven't hired me, nor have I accepted you as a client, so whatever you tell me isn't privileged—yet."

Ben took a moment to get the chronology straight in his mind, then launched into his narrative.

MacArthur listened without comment until Ben was through. "So the police—two detectives—called you in, gave you a Miranda warning, and said your friend Dr. Hinshaw had learned that one of his colleagues was involved in the drug ring they'd been trying to break. I'd infer that you weren't the only doctor they interviewed. Would you agree?"

"Probably," Ben replied.

"Hypothetically—I'm not asking you about guilt or innocence—but if you didn't kill Hinshaw, why are you so worried?"

Ben had thought of that, but hadn't voiced his concerns so far. Rachel might as well hear this, too, although he was certain she'd worry. "There was a patient some time ago that I treated in the emergency room and failed to save. There was a question in my mind whether a disgruntled member of that patient's family might be trying to harass me. But then, as these things continued, I changed my mind. I started to wonder if perhaps one of our surgeons was behind it. And I can't help believing Rick's death is connected to all this."

"Why do you say that about the surgeon?"

"Right after I hit town, I was contacted by an attorney and asked to review a case. I did, and there was obvious malpractice. The doctor's carrier settled, and since then he's seemed to have it in for me."

"And you think the doctor you mentioned is behind all this, including Hinshaw's death?"

Ben cleared his throat. "I don't know, but I wonder whether he might want to kill two birds with one stone—getting rid of Rick Hinshaw and framing me for the murder."

MacArthur tapped his front teeth with his pen and was silent for a while. Then he pulled open a desk drawer and removed a two-page form. "This is a contract for representation. There'll be a retainer involved." He scribbled a figure on a Post-It note and shoved it toward Ben. "Then, depending on how much work that follows, my fees will increase."

Ben was already pulling out his checkbook. "When I was thinking about representation, I realized you wouldn't come cheap. Then I tried to figure out the price of my freedom. I eventually reached the conclusion that it's priceless." After writing in MacArthur's name, he scribbled the amount, signed it, then tore out the check and handed it his new attorney. "Let's get started."

Rachel was quiet when they finally left MacArthur's office. Ben held open her car door. "Want to go get something to eat?"

"I think I'll go home, probably have leftovers, and get to bed early." She tried to muster a smile. "But thanks. I'll call you tonight or tomorrow. Okay?"

"Sure. And thanks for finding MacArthur for me. I think I'll feel a lot better with him on my side."

"Good." Rachel looked around, and since there appeared to be no one in the immediate area, she felt free to give Ben a hug and kiss as they parted.

On her way home, she put the numbers together once more. She didn't think they meant anything, but nevertheless it was troubling. According to what the detectives told Ben, Rick Hinshaw was shot and killed early Wednesday morning. Did Ben have an alibi for that time? She wasn't certain whether he'd been at his office or in surgery. But suppose no one could vouch for his whereabouts at that time? The attorney hadn't gone into the issue of his alibi, hadn't even asked him if he was guilty. What if he was the doctor involved in the drug ring? Could he have kept it hidden from Rachel?

Rachel couldn't see a reason for her fiancé to kill one of his best friends, and she had no clue that he was involved in the local drug ring. But, then again, her father had apparently started shooting up again while his family either never suspected it or turned a blind eye toward his drug use. Maybe she was too trusting. Perhaps others were as well.

She steered her car toward her home more through muscle memory than active volition while turning all this over in her mind. Was there any clue that Ben might be less than the perfect man he appeared?

Finally, as she pulled into her garage, Rachel decided to stop trying to come to a conclusion on her own. Instead, after she turned off the ignition, she bowed her head until it was resting on the steering wheel.

God, either give me a sign of Ben's innocence or bolster my faith to stand beside him through this. I can't do it on my own.

As she meditated, her mind scrolled through her interactions with Ben. Her memory stopped at the conversation she and Ben had while on their way to her mother's home to break the news to her about the death of her ex. "In a way, I'm glad my father's overdose was pretty cut-and-dried," she'd said. "Otherwise, I guess I'd be under suspicion."

"Why do you say that?" He had taken his eyes off the road for a moment to glance at her.

"What is it the police look for when they try to solve a crime—motive, means, and opportunity? Well, I'm a nurse. Putting a needle into a vein is something I do every day. I have access to IV drugs. And I don't have any way to prove where I was when Dad died."

"But you don't have any reason to want him dead."

"Oh, yes. I've thought more than once how nice it would be if Dad were dead."

"That's news to me," Ben said.

"Did you suspect my father had a drug problem?"

Ben was silent for a few seconds. "I suspected he'd done something bad, and one problem might be drug addiction. But I figured you'd tell me when you were ready."

"And would it have made a difference?"

"Of course not. I'm marrying you, so I get the whole family package—the bad as well as the good. If you had an uncle who was a drunk or a cousin in prison, I'd accept them—because I love you. And that includes everything that's contributed to who you are right now."

"Even my family situation," Rachel said.

"Frankly, your family situation seems … unusual, but when you think about it, mine isn't exactly typical. My mother and father died in a car crash when I was still in college. They were both only children, and I don't have any brothers or sisters, so what you see is what you get." He took a deep breath. "No, as I've told you, I'll take whatever your family is, so long as you're included in the package."

Rachel raised her head from the steering wheel as the memory faded away. Tears dampened her cheeks, and she used her fingers to wipe them away. Ben was ready to accept her and all she brought to the marriage. More than that, he didn't think the worst of her. She should do the same for him.

Ben had a dream Thursday night, but this wasn't the same one that had tortured him for months. In this nightmare, instead of Lawton Harrison, the man who lay on the gurney was Bill Gardner. Faceless doctors and nurses shuffled to and fro in a large room that was somehow familiar, but none of them stopped despite Ben's urgent plea for help. Finally, he tried to start an IV himself, but as soon as he put a tourniquet on the man's arm and tightened it, a needle and syringe appeared. The rubber tubing he'd used to bring up Gardner's vein vanished, and the contents of the syringe flooded into the man's veins, injected by an unseen hand.

Gardner took one deep breath, and let it out with a sigh. His body tensed, almost like a generalized rigor, then relaxed until he was like a man made from putty—lifeless and unmoving. Gardner's expression was the same one Ben had seen at the man's apartment. Had he been given a chance to save the life of the person who was soon to be his father-in-law? Ben pounded once on the man's chest, but before he could start cardiopulmonary resuscitation, two figures appeared beside him. Each took his biceps in a firm grip and moved him away from the corpse. The large black man said, "You've killed him." The other, a petite blonde, said, "You're under arrest for murder."

With a cry, Ben woke and flung aside the twisted sheets that held him. He sat up on the side of the bed, his pulse rapid, and drops of sweat dripping between his shoulder blades, feeling like an army of ants crawling on him. It was still dark outside, so he flipped on the lamp beside his bed. He felt foolish, but he looked around the bedroom to assure he was alone.

He'd wished on more than one occasion that the dream about trying to save the life of Lawton Harrison would stop torturing him. But the one that replaced it tonight was ten times worse. The bedside clock told him it was only four in the morning. He didn't have to get up yet, but Ben knew there was no need in trying to go back to sleep. It was too early or late, depending on how you looked at it, to call Rachel, although he would have given anything to have her sitting by his side.

What would Rachel do if she were here? There was no question in Ben's mind. She'd pray. Could he do that? He remembered being told God didn't keep score, which was good, because if He did, Ben would be on the losing end. His Christianity wasn't always the strongest, and without Rachel to guide him, he was on his own. Then he realized he wasn't truly alone—had never been. He bowed his head, both in acknowledgement and humility, and murmured, "God, I need Your help."

Rachel slept fitfully on Friday night. She awoke with a vague sense of dread, knowing there were things she needed to attend to, but more than that, fearful that the day probably held more surprises.

Sheila had told her again yesterday to take some time off. Rachel declined. "Thanks, but it's best that I come to work and stay busy. I don't want to sit at home and think about what's gone on—or worry about what might be coming next."

She was pretty certain trouble would find her, wherever she was and whatever she was doing.

Should she call Ben? Rachel decided he had enough on his mind. He'd contact her when he had time. Meanwhile, she filled a travel cup with coffee and set out for the hospital.

There she was met with the usual comments of, "I'm so sorry for your loss," and "Let us know what we can do for you." Rachel wasn't sure what to say in return. Maybe she should respond with "My father died with a needle in his arm. How can you fix that?" She settled on a simple, "Thanks."

Yesterday, Sheila offered Rachel sympathy and assistance. Today she simply made the nursing assignments and left everyone to go about their business. As they left the nurses' station, she whispered to Rachel, "Praying for you." And that was that.

As Rachel went about her duties, random thoughts ran through her head. Ben hadn't called her before she put her cell phone in her locker, but that wasn't unusual. At her lunch break, she'd look for a text message from him. If there was nothing, Rachel might call his office to see what his schedule was. At any rate, they would be together this weekend. They could talk about the situation then.

Rachel still had a hard time believing her father was dead. Was falling into the pit of drug addiction the reason her father had wanted money? On the one hand, it seemed like an enormous sum. On the other, she guessed illegal drugs cost a lot. She really had no idea. But whatever it cost, she would have given that much and more if her father had stayed clean.

Rachel was about to tell Sheila she was leaving for her lunch break when the light over the door of room 265 came on. This was one of her patients, so she decided to handle the call before leaving the floor. When she had checked vital signs that morning, she'd found Mrs. Merkle's blood pressure to be a bit low—not dangerous, but enough of a change to be a warning.

"Mrs. Merkle," Rachel had said, "I don't like the level of your blood pressure. I think I'd better call your surgeon."

"No, don't bother him. I feel okay, and I'm sure he'll be around later this morning."

When Rachel rechecked the woman after an hour or so, there'd been no change in her fast pulse and low blood pressure. Mrs. Merkel didn't seem shocky. Maybe her vitals were normal for the older patient. Nevertheless, Rachel planned to ask her relief nurse to watch the woman carefully.

When she walked through the door, she saw Mrs. Merkle hanging half out of bed, with her gown almost to her waist and her left hand holding on to the call button apparatus as though it were a lifeline.

The woman gave a wan smile. "I thought I could make it to the bathroom on my own. I guess not, though. I hate to bother you."

Rachel jerked the gown until Mrs. Merkle was appropriately covered. "Not a problem. Can you move?"

"I'll try." But it soon became apparent she wasn't strong enough to help Rachel. The woman was dead weight.

Rachel struggled and eventually moved Mrs. Merkle fully onto the bed. "Just lie back and let's have a look at you." A quick assessment of the force and rapidity of her pulse, and Rachel was now certain Mrs. Merkle was going into shock. Rachel would need reinforcements, so she reached for the nurse call button and pressed the tab that indicated an urgent request.

Within a few seconds, Sheila and another nurse, Joe, hurried into the room. After one look at Mrs. Merkle they swung into action.

"I'll get the cuff on her and check her blood pressure," Sheila said.

"She's not my patient," Joe said. "Remind me what operation she had and who her surgeon is."

Sheila didn't look up from the blood pressure cuff she was wrapping around Mrs. Merkle's arm. "She had an abdominal hysterectomy yesterday ... by Dr. Kasner."

Rachel pressed the control and raised the foot of the bed to place the patient in the shock position. "Is he in the hospital this morning?"

Joe had tied a tourniquet on Mrs. Merkle's arm opposite the one where Sheila worked, preparing to start a second IV. He had a bag of lactated Ringers solution ready to run in as soon as he got the line in.

Sheila finished taking Mrs. Merkle's blood pressure, shook her head, and pressed the button on the control that let her talk to the nurses' station. "Sherry, get us a surgeon in here stat."

"Which one?"

"Anyone you can find. STAT!"

When Ben dropped by Rachel's house on Friday evening, it was soon apparent she seemed preoccupied. "Something bothering you?"

She looked up at him. "Lots of things."

He brushed a stray strand of hair from her forehead and kissed it. "Want to tell me about it?"

She led him into the living room where they sat in their usual places, side by side on the sofa. "A woman Dr. Kasner operated on yesterday went into shock on the ward today. We grabbed the first available surgeon, Dr. McLelland, and he started treatment, which included rushing her into surgery to look for internal bleeding. While we were getting her ready to go, he called around trying to locate Dr. Kasner, but no luck."

"So, who was Kasner checked out to?"

"That's just it. No one. McLelland opened her up and found a tie had come loose from an ovarian artery. After the surgery and some blood replacement, the woman will be okay, but …"

"Yeah, but where was Kasner? And why didn't he have someone checking on his post-op patient?"

"Not to mention, why was he doing a gynecologic case in the first place? And couldn't that have been done using an endoscope?" Rachel shifted on the sofa. "I realize that wasn't the way general surgeons did it when Dr. Kasner trained, but hasn't he kept up with advances in the field? If he keeps practicing like this, he's liable to kill someone."

Ben shook his head. "As for the first question, I don't know why he did the case himself, but this isn't the first time I've seen him perform surgeries other docs would send to a specialist. And, yes, using endoscopic control reduces the chances of bleeding and infection. But apparently, Kasner still practices the way he was trained thirty years ago."

"Anyway, the woman's all right now, and Dr. McLelland said he'd keep checking on her."

"I'm glad someone is caring for her and she'll be okay," Ben said. "But the question remains—"

"Where was Dr. Kasner?" She gave him another hug. Ben smiled at her. "I came over to spend time with you. Let's not waste any more on Kasner."

Rachel's cell phone rang. The caller ID said Carlyle PD. She frowned before answering.

"Ms. Gardner, this is Detective Murchison of the Carlyle

Police Department. Sorry to call you so late, but I wonder if we could talk with you a bit—maybe tomorrow."

"Maybe. Is this about my father's death?" She pulled the phone away from her ear so Ben could hear the conversation. "Why are you still looking into that?"

"In a routine search of your father's apartment, our people found a million-dollar life insurance policy."

Rachel nodded. "Yes. Dad took it out shortly after he and Mom were married. I presume she's still the beneficiary."

"No, he apparently changed it after the divorce."

Rachel felt her gut contract. "And what was the change?"

"You're the new beneficiary." The detective paused for a second. "Let me confirm something. You're a nurse, aren't you?"

She remembered something she'd heard a doctor say about expert testimony. That was probably applicable here. Just answer the question without embellishment. "Yes."

"So injecting something into a vein would be relatively easy for you."

"I … I don't think I'll answer any more questions," Rachel said.

"You don't have any choice, but maybe we should do this face to face," Murchison said. "Tomorrow's Saturday. Can you be at the Carlyle PD about ten tomorrow morning?"

Ben reached over and took the phone from Rachel, who didn't protest. "This is Dr. Ben Merrick, Ms. Gardner's fiancé. We'll both be there tomorrow morning. And we'll be accompanied by an attorney."

7

Without thinking it through, Ben pulled out Bob MacArthur's card. The attorney had written his home and cell phone numbers on the back. He dialed the cell number without hesitation. Ben figured that attorneys, like doctors, got calls at all hours. While the call was ringing, Ben wondered if the attorney was home on a Friday night or at dinner or a movie? And would he even answer his cell?

MacArthur answered on the third ring. "Dr. Merrick, I presume there's something urgent that triggered this call."

"I'll tell you what I'm often told when I get calls like this. I'm sorry to phone you at home. But I've got a problem, and I need your help."

There was a pause, then the phone picked up the faint sound of a door closing. "I've excused myself from the dinner table. My wife probably won't be too happy with you, but frankly, I don't much care for what she's cooked tonight, so I won't fuss. Now tell me what's going on? Did you get another call from the Freeman police?"

"No, this one came from the Carlyle PD. And I'll need to give you some background about my fiancé's father and his death from a drug overdose."

MacArthur listened without comment as Ben told him the details, ending with the call from Detective Murchison.

"I don't want Rachel walking in there tomorrow without legal representation. It sounds to me like she's under more suspicion for her father's murder than I was for Rick Hinshaw's death. I know I've paid you a retainer, and that's fine. But—"

"Let me stop you there. You want me to represent Rachel. Right?"

"Yes."

"I agree with you that she probably needs it more than you. Ordinarily, I'd say I can't take her on as a client, but she was in my sister's class in nursing school. Suppose we do it this way. I'll represent her, so long as there's no conflict with your case. If there is, we'll decide what to do then."

"Great," Ben said. "We were due tomorrow morning—"

"I remember. You're scheduled to meet Detective Murchison tomorrow at ten. Yes, I'll be there, and I know the location. Now don't worry about the call." He chuckled. "I'll pretend it was a terrible thing to be called away from my wife's dinner."

"Please extend my apologies to her."

MacArthur laughed. "You'll have to meet her after this is all over. When you see her, you'll understand why it doesn't matter to me whether she's a good cook."

Ben ended the call and turned to Rachel. "Could you hear most of that?"

"I could. I'm glad to have a lawyer like Bob MacArthur on my side. And his wife must be extremely beautiful."

"Not as beautiful as you," Ben said, and he gave Rachel a sweet kiss.

On Saturday morning, when Rachel walked into the Carlyle police station with Ben, she found Attorney Robert

MacArthur already standing at the front desk, chatting with easy familiarity with the policeman who sat there. The lawyer didn't seem at all upset to be kept waiting. Of course, he probably started the meter when he left his office. She supposed that one of the things attorneys did a lot, especially those involved in courtroom proceedings, was wait.

MacArthur walked over and exchanged handshakes with them both. Then he turned to Rachel. "Give me a dollar."

She frowned, but dug in her purse and handed him a crumpled bill. "And this is—?"

"Now you're officially my client. Anything you tell me is privileged information. If there's anything the detective asks that you're unsure about, check with me before answering. And if it's private, you and I will go off in a corner and discuss it. Clear?"

Rachel nodded.

"We're all here," MacArthur said to the policeman at the desk. "Shall we go on in?"

"Sure." He nodded at the entrance to the offices and buzzed them in.

MacArthur opened the door and gestured for Rachel and Ben to precede him down the hall and into the squad room. An older man in a suit that seemed too heavy for the season rose from his desk. His tie was askew, his shoes were scuffed, and he'd missed a spot while shaving that morning.

"Ms. Gardner, this is Detective Arthur Murchison. Art, the man with her is her fiancé, Dr. Ben Merrick." Turning to his two clients, he smiled. "Don't be fooled by appearances. This is one of the sharpest men on the force." He spoke to Murchison. "Where do you want to hold this meeting?"

Murchison gave what might have served as a grin, then got up from his desk and gestured toward a nearby interview room. "We'll go in here."

As they filed into the room, which was surprisingly like the one Ben had seen at the Freeman police station, they were joined by a young man wearing a knit shirt, chinos, and loafers. He removed a baseball cap to reveal somewhat disarrayed blond hair.

"My partner, Kellen Rich," Murchison said. "Ms. Gardner, Dr. Merrick. Their lawyer, Robert MacArthur."

Rich nodded all around and took the chair next to Murchison. The older detective asked permission to record the interview, and after assent from MacArthur, he turned on the recorder. Rachel noted he didn't give her the standard, "You have the right to remain silent ..." Miranda warning. She hoped that was a good sign.

Murchison looked at Rachel. "Let's start with your father's drug habit. What can you tell us about it?"

"My mother kept her marital problems under cover while I was at home. After I left for nursing school, she divorced my father. It was only then that I learned he had a problem with drug addiction. Subsequently, I heard from my father on several occasions that he had kicked the habit, but my mother remained unconvinced. When he asked Ben for money—lots of money—I worried that Dad had gotten himself in trouble, probably with drug use. Like so many family members I'm sure you encounter, I refused to believe it until the evidence couldn't be ignored, finding him dead, a needle and syringe still in his arm." She clutched her hands in her lap. "That's all I know about his drug habit."

"And the insurance policy?" Rich asked, in a voice that sounded older than his appearance.

"I knew that he took out two large policies years ago. I was a child, but I was told that mother was the beneficiary of one. The other was key man insurance, payable to Joe Durbin, who ran Dad's auto dealership." She frowned.

"I think Durbin had a similar policy with my father as beneficiary."

"If your father needed money to pay off his drug debts, why do you suppose he didn't take money—either legitimately or surreptitiously—from the dealership?" Murchison asked. "According to what we've seen so far, it was doing well."

"I've wondered about that myself. I think that, his drug habit aside, my father was an honorable man. Even after his divorce, he kept up with my mother and made certain she had everything she needed. And I don't think he'd ever rob his own company—too many people worked for him, and he took that responsibility seriously."

"When did you know he changed the beneficiary on his insurance policy?" Rich asked.

"I didn't know about it until you told me." She turned to look at MacArthur. "And, besides, doesn't suicide void the policy?"

"It varies with the policy, but most of them vest after two or three years, so they pay for loss of life, whatever the cause," MacArthur said. He looked at Murchison and pointed to the recorder. "But be sure to note that not only did Ms. Gardner not know she was the new beneficiary of her father's will, but she was under the impression that the policy was voided by Mr. Gardner's suicide."

Rich addressed MacArthur directly. "It's easy enough for your client to say that after the fact. But she had a million reasons to want her father dead. She's a nurse, so finding a vein for injection is fairly easy for her. And she's a family member, so he'd let her into the apartment."

Rachel's voice was filled with outrage. "You can't really be considering that I'd kill my father."

"Let me jump in here." Ben half-rose from his chair.

"No, let me." MacArthur turned to the older detective.

"Art, let's cut to the chase. Do you have any reason to believe Bill Gardner's death was anything but a self-administered injection of a lethal dose of drug?"

Murchison was quiet for a moment before he shook his head. "No. Everything points to that. The apartment was locked from the inside. The only fingerprints on the syringe were Gardner's."

"Then why are we here?" MacArthur asked the older detective.

"I wanted to take one more shot. Sometimes we get lucky and the person who thinks they've committed the perfect murder breaks down when we stare across the table at them." He glanced at the case folder in front of him.

"So this case is closed," MacArthur said.

"Actually, this case might stay open for a while, but not because we think your client did the injecting. We think Gardner might have injected himself with Gray Death. And we'd like to know where he got it."

The meeting broke up soon after. Outside the police station, Rachel turned to Ben. "What's Gray Death?"

"I've heard of it, but I can't tell you a lot." Ben consulted MacArthur. "Do you know much about it?"

"Unfortunately, I do. It's fairly new, but as a criminal defense attorney, I've had to learn."

"What is it?" Rachel asked.

"Years ago, the drugs of choice were marijuana and cocaine, but those didn't give enough bang for the buck. Then morphine and opioids like hydrocodone were popular. After that, a few entertainers started using fentanyl for the high it gave. The Michael Jackson case comes to mind." MacArthur took in a deep breath and blew it out slowly. "Recently, someone came up with the idea of mixing heroin, fentanyl, and a synthetic opioid called U-47700 with an elephant tranquilizer, carfentanil, hoping to give a really maximum high."

"And did it," Rachel asked.

"Well, yes, if you like to gamble with your life," MacArthur said. "It can kill with a single dose. So, if Gray Death is popping up now, I suppose it's more important than ever for the police to find the source and close down the pipeline."

On the brief ride to Freeman, Ben glanced at Rachel. "I meant to ask you about the funeral service for your dad. Have you and your mother decided where it's going to be held?"

"Mom said that when they were first married, my father would sometimes go with her to what she considered 'their' church. Then he began to use the excuse of needing to be at the auto dealership on Sundays, even though they didn't open until noon. When I left for college, their marriage was about to go down the tubes, so he quit pretending. Mom continued to go, and her church is where the service will be held."

"Any other details?"

"Mom and I talked with the pastor and gave him a short list of hymns and a couple of Scriptures. We decided to put the service off until later next week, though, and the funeral director has agreed." Rachel took a deep breath. "As we heard this morning, there won't be an investigation into the death—except trying to find out where the stuff he injected came from—but I don't think it's a bad idea to let things quiet down before the service."

"No, I think you're right. We want things to settle down."

And we still don't know who's behind these incidents aimed at me. I'd like to get to the bottom of that before they escalate.

8

The smell of coffee perking woke Ben on Sunday morning. After a few misses, he had finally mastered the habit of loading his coffeemaker the evening before. Sometimes he still forgot to push the button to set the auto-brew function, but last night, thankfully, he had remembered. Nothing like fresh coffee to help him get going in the morning. For the first few seconds he was awake, Ben wondered why he was climbing out of bed this early on a day when he wasn't on call and had no one in the hospital? Then he remembered. This was Sunday, and he was accompanying Rachel to church.

Ben's church attendance had started a rapid slide as soon as he left home, hitting absolute bottom by the time he began his surgery residency. He knew his behavior was common among his peers, and it didn't worry him. But shortly after setting up his practice in Freeman, he'd started seeing Rachel regularly, and things changed. There were weekends when professional duties kept him from church, but when possible, Ben spent most Sunday mornings with Rachel at the First Community Church. Sometimes he found his mind wandering during the service, but at other times, he actually followed the message. If church attendance was important to Rachel, he wanted to go with her. He wished he could be as close to God as she was. He was trying.

As he dressed, he reminded himself that later today he needed to follow up on Dr. Kasner's absence—maybe after lunch. He wasn't a fan of the older physician, but he wanted to know why the doctor had pulled his vanishing act when he had a post-op patient in the recovery room.

Opinions in Freeman varied about Kasner. Although doctors and nurses generally considered Kasner a joke, some of his patients seemed to love him. The stories of the times he snatched moribund patients from the jaws of death had reached the level of folk-legend, although Ben was certain these had been embellished over the years. The more objective opinions came from the younger physicians in the community. Perhaps it was because they hadn't seen Kasner in his early years. What they saw now was a surgeon who practiced what had at one time been state-of-the-art, but what was now hopelessly outdated medicine. And worse, he didn't seem to care.

It was Ben's considered opinion, admittedly colored by his battles with the older surgeon, that if Kasner couldn't keep up with advances in his specialty, he should retire from practice. But apparently there were people, including a number on the hospital board and a few senior physicians, who recalled the doctor's prowess during his younger days and refused to notice the change. So Kasner kept rolling on, flattening anyone who disagreed with him.

Ben finished his coffee, took a last bite of his toasted bagel, and headed out the door. He'd think about Dr. Kasner later. Right now, he needed to pick up Rachel for church.

"I appreciate your taking the time to talk to us." Detective Murchison uncrossed his leg and pulled out his notepad. "I know Sunday can be a busy day at an auto dealership, and as manager I guess you have a lot to do."

Joe Durbin shrugged and looked out the glass wall of his office at the activity on the showroom floor. "You'd think that the death of the owner would make things grind to a halt here, but if anything, it's brought more people in—even if it's become common knowledge that he died of an overdose." He tilted his chair forward and leaned his elbows on the desk. "Not only was he popular in the community. Everyone who worked here loved him."

Murchison didn't reply. He looked at Rich, sitting in the chair next to him. Today, perhaps in deference to it being Sunday, the other detective had "dressed up" with a sport coat and pressed jeans.

"Mr. Durbin," Rich said. "Was there anyone here who might have contributed to Mr. Gardner's death? Specifically, anyone who could have been supplying him with drugs?"

Durbin's answer came after only a moment's reflection. "No, I can't imagine anyone doing that. All our employees loved Bill Gardner. He was fair—more than fair—to everyone here, from me down to the janitor who cleaned up after we turned out the lights."

"Care to give an example?" Murchison asked.

Durbin leaned back in his chair. "Sure. Recently Chuck, one of our mechanics, told Bill his son needed surgery, but for some reason the insurance company wouldn't cover it. To show you the kind of man Bill Gardner was, he called the company three or four times, finally ending up talking with the company's president. When that was unsuccessful and the insurance company wouldn't budge, Bill told Chuck he would cosign a note for whatever it took, and they'd work out repayment later. Incidentally, last week the company reversed their stand and said they'd cover the procedure."

Rich made a note. "When we went through Mr. Gardner's papers, we found he carried a rather large life insurance policy. Did you know about that?"

"I think he may have mentioned it once or twice." Durbin shrugged. "I believe he took that out years ago."

"Along with that policy we found another one in his papers here in his office," Rich continued. "It was also for a million dollars. Did you know about that one too?"

Durbin nodded. "I believe Bill took that out shortly after we opened the dealership. I've been with him from the beginning, and if you look in my safe, you'll find a similar policy on me. Bill said that if either of us died, the other one would need the money to keep the dealership operating until they decided how to move forward."

"And have you decided?"

Durbin didn't answer immediately. He pulled a handkerchief from his hip pocket and wiped his eyes. "No." His voice seemed choked with emotion.

Ben stopped his car outside Rachel's house. "Are you sure you don't want lunch?"

"Thanks, but today I want to spend time alone. You understand, don't you?"

"Sure. I'll pick up something at the hospital while I nose around and see what I can find out about Kasner." Ben squeezed her hand.

"Let me know what you find out." Rachel opened her door. "I'll make a grilled cheese or a peanut-butter sandwich. Maybe watch a totally worthless program on TV. Then, later this afternoon, I might call my mother to see if she wants to talk. I'm worried she still hasn't processed this fully."

Ben made certain Rachel was safely inside her house before he pulled away from the curb. As he drove, he pondered his next move. Although most doctors preferred to make rounds first thing on Sunday morning, others postponed their patient visits until mid-afternoon. Maybe someone would be around who could tell Ben about the elusive Dr. Kasner. If he didn't find anyone who knew, he would make some phone calls. And he could pick up a tuna sandwich and milk at the Food Court while he was at the hospital.

Mindful of Rick Hinshaw's recent death, Ben looked around him frequently as he walked from his car to the hospital entrance. His first stop was the surgeon's lounge. He found the room empty. Ben walked into the adjoining dressing room, and it, too, was uninhabited. He was about to walk out when anesthesiologist Art McNabb came in and started to shed his sweat-stained scrub clothes.

"Have an emergency case?" Ben asked his colleague.

"Yep. Miles Kirwin had a patient with a ruptured ectopic pregnancy. Managed to pull the patient through, but it was a tough one. He's still in the recovery room with her."

"Do you have another case after this?"

Art tossed the last of his scrub clothing into the basket and grabbed a towel. "Nope. With Rick's death, the rest of the anesthesiologists are busy, so I haven't gotten much rest. I was here most of the night, so I plan to go home and get some sleep. But I'll shower first."

"Sounds like you're exhausted, but can you spare a couple of minutes of your time?"

Art didn't seem the least bit self-conscious, standing next to the shower stall in his underwear, a towel draped over his shoulder. "Sure."

"Rachel told me that one of Dr. Kasner's post-op patients

went into shock on Friday, and no one could find him when they put out a call."

"Yeah, I heard about that. Dr. McLelland took care of the lady. When it was all over, his efforts to get Kasner to answer were negative, so the hospital administrator called the police and asked them to do a welfare check at the man's home."

"He lives alone, doesn't he?"

"Yeah."

"And?"

Art shrugged. "You must be the only surgeon in town who doesn't know.

"I've been busy. Know what?"

"The police found Kasner on the floor of his house, unconscious. He must have gone home after his case, then suffered a massive stroke." The anesthesiologist pointed vaguely upward. "He's on 4 South in medical intensive care. And it doesn't look good."

After a light lunch of cheese and crackers, Rachel decided to relax in her recliner for a bit. She sat down and pushed the button on the TV remote, thinking she'd watch a DIY program, maybe combine a bit of learning with her rest.

She channel-surfed until she found a show about remodeling a home. Rachel stretched out and closed her eyes. The images weren't important. She'd listen to the audio. The next thing she knew she was awakened by the ringing of her phone, while the TV nattered in the background with some commercial about yard tractors.

She yawned and looked at the time on her cell phone. She'd been asleep for almost an hour. Shaking her head, she muted the TV and answered the call.

"Rachel, did I wake you?" her mother asked.

For some reason, Rachel—like most people—answered in the negative. She wasn't certain why. Surely she deserved a nap on Sunday afternoon, but for some reason she hated her mother to "catch" her sleeping. "No, Mom. I intended to call you later. What's up?"

Her mother's voice caught for a moment. "I never thought I'd miss Bill. I hated his drug habit, but nothing I could do was enough to get him to change, I guess."

"I loved him too. Even with his faults."

"Oh, there were times before our divorce when I thought how simple it would be if Bill were to take too much of whatever drug he was using at the moment," she said. "But I never acted on it."

Rachel started to say she'd had the same thought, but decided not to pursue it. "I guess no one would blame someone in your position for feeling that way. You worked hard to keep things normal around our house, even when they weren't. But you managed somehow."

They had been chatting for about ten minutes when Rachel heard a tone in her ear. She looked at the caller ID. "Ben's calling, Mom. Can I get back with you?"

"No need to bother. I only wanted to touch base with my daughter. I have one of my friends coming over soon. I'll be fine. I'll talk to you tomorrow, if that's all right." She paused. "Tell Ben hello for me, and thank him for all his help."

Rachel punched the button to end one call and answer the other. "Ben, I was talking with my mother. She said to tell you hello."

"Is she doing better?"

"I think she's managing," Rachel said. "Now what did you find out about Dr. Kasner?"

"The reason no one could find him was that he was at

home, unconscious. He apparently had a massive stroke. The police responded to a welfare check, went to his house, and discovered him lying on the floor. He's in medical ICU at the hospital, still in a coma."

"On life support?"

"His respirations were a little bit under the lower limits of normal, so they intubated him and put him on a ventilator, hoping the additional oxygen might help," Ben said. "The only relative anyone could find was his sister, who's coming in late today from Kansas City."

"Wow. I know you've had a contentious relationship with Dr. Kasner, but … Honey, we should pray for him."

"Actually, I already have," Ben said.

"It sounds as though he won't be able to function, certainly not for a while and maybe never. So, what will his staff do about his patients?"

"They'll refer them elsewhere if they call. And the surgeons in town will cover those cases he already has scheduled."

"Has anyone called you?" Rachel asked.

"Not yet. I guess there was some question about whether I'd be willing to help since I'd had trouble with Kasner. But after I found out what had happened, I called Dr. McLelland. He's the one who's putting this together." He paused. "I told him I'd be glad to do my part."

"I'm happy you did," Rachel said. "Dr. Kasner wasn't very loveable—"

Ben finished the sentence for her. "But he was a human."

9

When Rachel arrived on Two North on Monday morning, she didn't see the head nurse, Sheila Britton. That was unusual. Sheila was generally the first one there, talking with the night crew, making certain everything was in order, preparing for the morning report when she'd make nursing assignments for the day.

When Joe, another nurse who usually worked the day shift, walked up, Rachel commented on her absence. "Do you know where Sheila is?"

"No, I expected she'd be here. To tell the truth, she's been one of the few constants on this ward since I've been working here."

By that time, almost the entire team—nurses, aides, technicians—had gathered at the front desk. When the phone rang, Shirley, the ward clerk, answered it, then held it out to Rachel. "It's for you."

Rachel frowned. Her mother and Ben were the only two people who had her permission to call her at work, and either would only phone if it was a dire emergency. Her pulse pounded in her ears. Rachel felt a tightness in her throat. Her hand trembled when she reached for the phone. "This is Rachel Gardner."

"Rachel, this is Sheila. I was in my car on the way to the

hospital when I was T-boned by a panel van. The fire department cut me out of the vehicle a moment ago, and I had to almost fight to get my cell phone from them."

"Sheila, are you—"

"Listen, because they may take this phone away from me any minute. I'm okay, although, in addition to the expected bumps and bruises, it looks to me like my left arm is fractured. They're transporting me to Freeman Memorial, but I don't know when I'll have a chance to call anyone to tell them what happened. In the meantime—"

There was a murmur of voices in the background followed by Sheila's pleading voice.

"Wait! I need another ten seconds! Please!"

Rachel pictured her friend virtually wrestling her cell phone away. When Sheila came on the line again, her words tumbled out. "You're in charge. Call down to nursing service, explain what happened, then have them send a floater to take up the slack. I—"

The noises were brief this time, followed by a man's voice on the call. "Your friend is okay, but I may have to spank her if she reaches for this phone again with her good arm. Now we're on our way to the hospital." A click signaled the end of the conversation.

Rachel turned to the group assembled around her. She looked down the hall and saw a couple of call lights on already. "Sheila has been in an accident. She's okay other than a fractured arm. Let's get to work, and I'll tell you more when I know it."

On Monday morning, Ben was seeing his second patient of the day, an elderly gentleman with a leg ulcer that was slow to heal, when Betty tapped on the door of the exam room before opening it. "Dr. Merrick, the ER is on the line. They say they'll hold, but they need to talk with you."

"Fine. Would you show Mr. Tompkins how to dress this ulcer? Then give him dressing material and the sample tube of antibiotic ointment that's on the table. After that, please set him up for a blood sugar and CBC, with a return visit in about a week." He looked at the patient. "Any questions?"

When the man shook his head no, Ben hurried into his office, picked up the phone, and punched the blinking, lighted button. "This is Dr. Merrick."

"Hey, Ben. This is Roger Mann in the ER. I need your opinion about a patient who came in this morning."

"I thought Carl Rosser had this shift."

"He did," the ER doctor replied. "But he had to cancel at the last minute, so I stayed over to cover the first half of his shift, and Mo Patel will come on early to handle the second half."

Ben wondered what kind of situation made Carl cancel. Meanwhile, Roger filled him in on a man who'd been brought in after a two-car crash. "The collision was bad enough that he's got a significant bruise across his lap. That doesn't worry me, but he also has left upper quadrant tenderness with a bit of pain in the left shoulder. His pressure's down a little, but it's still within normal limits. I'm wondering about a mild fracture of the splenic capsule."

Spleen injuries were always a possibility in cases of trauma such as this, and emergency room doctors were especially wary of them. "What's your plan?"

"His hemoglobin-hematocrit look okay right now, but I'll repeat an H&H every hour or so, as well as monitoring his vital signs. I've sent him for a CT of the abdomen, which should clarify the diagnosis. But—"

"You'd like me to look at him, either way." Ben knew it was better for two doctors to send out a patient like this than for one to make the decision and then have the man return with undeniable signs of a splenic injury. "Why don't I come over in a couple of hours? The abdominal CT will be done by then, you'll have serial H&Hs to see if he's bleeding, and we can make the decision together. Call me earlier if you need me. Okay?"

Ben left his office to tell his receptionist he would be leaving for the hospital in a couple of hours. He only had two more patients to see this morning anyway, so maybe he'd get away even earlier. If the patient in the ER didn't require surgery, he probably should take a few minutes to go by and see Dr. Kasner. *Of course, he won't know I was there ... but I will.*

Rachel worked so hard to keep things moving on Two North that she didn't even think about a lunch break. The nurse sent up by the supervisor pitched in and was soon functioning as though she'd been working on that ward for years. Call lights kept going on until, at one time, the entire hallway looked like someone had strung white Christmas tree lights above all the doors. But through it all, the nurses, aides, technicians, and ward clerk kept things moving.

Rachel swept a lock of brown hair out of her eyes and looked at the clock above the nurses' station. This shift was almost over, and the end of this day couldn't come a moment too soon for her.

As she entered vital signs on the chart of one of her patients, Rachel wondered why Sheila had called her to take over. She could as easily called the hospital's nursing supervisor directly. Maybe it was because Rachel had worked there almost as long as Sheila. She knew the routine, was familiar with the ins and outs peculiar to Two North, its patient population, and the doctors who most often had patients there.

Eventually, Rachel gave the report to the nurse who relieved her, making certain there were no questions left hanging. By the time she finished, everyone on the day shift had left. She wanted nothing more than to head for the nurses' lounge, slip off her shoes, and collapse onto the sofa. But Rachel knew that if she did that, she'd fall fast asleep. She needed to retrieve her cell phone, head for home, and wait for Ben's call at the end of his day. But first of all, she needed to check on Sheila.

Ben agreed with the ER doctor and the radiologist that there was no evidence of rupture of the spleen or a tear in its capsule. The patient's vital signs had remained stable, as had his blood work. The pain in his abdomen and shoulder were attributable to the force of the crash—probably pressure from the seat belt. "You're a lucky man," Ben said to the man. "The accident that totaled your car was bad, but it could have been worse. You can replace things. You can never replace people."

After leaving the ER, he took the elevator to the fourth floor, and even though he didn't usually admit patients to the medical ICU, Ben had no trouble locating the wing and finding the room where Dr. Kasner lay. He had seen Kasner in the operating suite, occasionally encountered him in medical meetings, but the man lying in the bed looked different to Ben than he had in those circumstances. Then he'd been a doctor. Now, he was an older man hanging on to life.

Kasner had been intubated—that is, there was a tube in his windpipe, inserted through the mouth—and a machine at the bedside chuffed rhythmically, pumping air into his lungs.

The complexes represented by the green lines on a machine above Kasner's head showed his heartbeat to be so slow that Ben expected them to stop any moment. An IV dripped into a vein in his left hand, and a tube snaked out from beneath the covers to a bag containing a few inches of dark yellow liquid. It was like viewing a preparation in physiology class, rather than a human being barely hanging on to life.

There was no one else in the room. Kasner certainly didn't know Ben was here. There was no way to record this visit, nor did Ben need to, but he felt he should do something while he was here. The man on the bed had caused him nothing but trouble since shortly after he set up his practice in Freeman. But he was a person. And, as Ben had said moments before, "You can never replace people."

Ben reached out and touched Kasner's forehead. With his hand there, he bowed his head and murmured a prayer for this doctor whom he had considered an enemy. Perhaps he was still an enemy ... but as Rachel would say, God still loved him.

Rachel called down to the emergency room to find Sheila. Doctors might play the "doctor card" to cut through red tape, but she'd found that nurse-to-nurse requests also got results. One of the nurses from the day shift was still around, and she told Rachel the bone in Sheila's arm had to be pinned to get it to heal in normal position, so she'd been taken into surgery.

"The orthopedist was delayed a bit getting here to do the procedure, so your friend is probably still in the recovery room," the nurse said.

"And I guess she'll go to Two North afterward. I'll see if I can sneak in and say a few words to her while she's still in recovery. Thanks."

Rachel hurried to the surgical recovery room, which was on the first floor of the hospital, around the corner from the surgical suite. She ignored the "staff only" sign on the door—after all, she was hospital staff, she reasoned—and entered the numeric code she'd seen one of her colleagues use a few months ago. At the time, she wasn't certain why the numbers seemed familiar, until she realized they represented Ben's birthday. Apparently, the code was unchanged, because the door swung open.

It didn't take her long to spot Sheila, her left arm in a cast and elevated on two pillows. Rachel was on her way to see her friend when a nurse wearing a scrub dress and name tag stopped her.

"May I help you?"

Rachel realized she was an interloper in this part of the hospital, but she decided to try nurse-to-nurse communication. It had worked for her once today. She realized she was still wearing her name pin, currently covered by the white coat she'd donned when leaving the ward. She opened the coat to make certain her nursing smock and name plate showed. "I'm Rachel Gardner. I'm a nurse on Two North, and I wanted to check on Sheila Britton before you moved her out."

The recovery room nurse gave the briefest of smiles. "You can say hi, but she's still groggy from the anesthetic. So, keep it short." She started to hurry away, then turned. "We'll send her to your unit as soon as a bed opens up."

Rachel noted her friend's eyes were open, but she seemed to have a bit of trouble tracking. "Sheila, I'm here."

"Uh huh," Sheila mumbled. "Did it … go … okay without … me?"

"It went fine. Is there anything I can get you?"

Sheila's eyes closed, and for a moment Rachel thought she was asleep. Then she roused. "Nope. Neighbors … will—"

She closed her eyes again, and this time a gentle snore indicated sleep had overtaken her.

Rachel had the name of Sheila's neighbors, an older couple who lived in the apartment next to her friend's. She'd call them and explain why Sheila wouldn't be home for a day or two. She was certain they'd bring in her mail and papers. Fortunately, there were no pets to care for.

The other nurse walked up behind Rachel. "She asleep?"

"Yes. I'll let her neighbors know she's in the hospital, so they can keep an eye on her apartment." Rachel turned toward the door. "Thanks for letting me in."

As she exited into the hall, Rachel reflected that if something happened to her, she had Ben. And, in her mind, that made all the difference.

Ben's afternoon in the office held no surprises, which was fine with him. He had enough on his plate now— the death of Rachel's father, his friend Rick's murder, and his prime opponent in the medical community lying comatose in the hospital.

"Anything more?" he asked his nurse as he prepared to leave the office.

"No, you're clear."

There was one consultation at the hospital Ben needed to take care of. It was just as well, because his car seemed to head toward Freeman Memorial of its own accord. For a while his life could be expressed by three sides of a triangle: the office, the hospital, and Rachel's house. Lately, that triangle had changed shape to a parallelogram, adding the road from Freeman to Carlyle and the home of Rachel's mother. His prospective father-in-law had lived there as well, of course, but

Ben had only met the man face-to-face a couple of times while he was alive. He regretted that, although perhaps there was nothing he could have done to change the outcome of that scenario.

After he'd finished with his consultation, Ben decided to visit Kasner's room again. He didn't know why, but he felt drawn there. When he reached the medical ICU, someone walked out of Kasner's room.

Ben was about to turn away when he heard Carl Rosser's voice. "I thought that was you," the ER doctor said.

"Hi. I thought I'd drop by to see if Dr. Kasner's condition has improved. Been here long?"

Carl hesitated, but finally answered. "I've been here several times during the day. His sister will be in from Kansas City later, but I didn't think he should be alone."

"That's kind of you." *And a bit out of character.*

10

Rachel sat in the rear booth of one of their favorite restaurants, leaning forward as Ben talked with her about his visit to Kasner's room. "You saw Carl Rosser there?"

"I imagine that others on the medical staff came by, although I didn't really expect Carl to be one of them." He picked up his glass and sipped his iced tea. "What really surprised me was that Carl said he'd been there off and on all day."

They paused as the entrees were served and their glasses topped off. Rachel added sweetener and stirred as she thought about what to say. When she spoke, her voice was so soft, Ben had to lean across the table to hear her.

"Do you have any idea why Dr. Kasner seemed to have a lot of doctors and prominent people in this town under his thumb?"

"No, but I suspect he's been here long enough to know where the bodies are buried, to use an old cliché." Ben cut a piece of his steak, chewed, and swallowed. "But let's put that aside. You said you had an unusual day. Tell me about it."

Rachel neglected her chef's salad while she told Ben about Sheila's accident and what transpired afterward.

"Is she okay?" he asked.

"Apparently so. She'll go from the recovery room to Two

North, so I should be able to talk with her tomorrow when I get to work."

"Does that mean that you'll be filling in for her for a while?"

"I doubt it. She probably called me because I'd been there a long time and had filled in for her a few times. She and I started work at Freeman Memorial about the same time." She stabbed a piece of lettuce and a part of a tomato wedge and held them up as she completed her answer. "We'll see what the nursing supervisor does about this tomorrow."

Ben was silent for a moment. "Have you heard anything more from the detectives in Carlyle? I suppose they're still working on finding out who was your father's supplier."

"No news," Rachel said. "I was hoping they'd have something to report before my father's funeral." She put down her fork and dabbed at her lips with a napkin. "And I guess that's the next big thing to get ready for."

On Tuesday morning, Ben was scheduled for a couple of surgical cases. As he finished the second one, an inguinal hernia repair, the phone in the operating room rang.

The circulating nurse answered, jotted down a message, and hung up. "Dr. Merrick, that was your office. When you finish, they'd like you to call."

Ben didn't spend much time wondering what it was they wanted. He'd had calls like this before. Usually they involved passing on a message that was too long or involved to trust to whoever in the OR answered, or too important to wait until he returned to the office.

After he'd finished with the case, he used the phone in the

surgeons' lounge to reach his office. "Earline, what do you have for me?"

"We got a call from a woman who said she needed to talk with you as soon as possible," the secretary responded.

"Was she a patient? A family member?"

"No. This was a Ms. Sarah Hunsaker. She said she was Dr. Kasner's sister, and she wanted to talk with you ASAP."

"Okay." He would be happy to meet the woman, although he couldn't figure out why there was this much urgency. "Do you have a number, or is she in Dr. Kasner's ICU room?"

"I have her cell phone. She said if you'd call her, she'd like to meet you in the Food Court and talk with you over coffee."

Wonder why she doesn't want to meet in Kasner's room? I guess she's ready to get out of the ICU. "Okay. Give me that number. And I should be back before noon."

Ben phoned Ms. Hunsaker, who answered on the first ring. "I've heard about you from my brother. He mentioned you a lot, which is why I wanted to speak with you."

What could she possibly have heard from Kasner? Nothing good. "We're all sorry to hear what happened to your brother. What can I do for you?"

"As I said, my brother talked about you a lot, and although he didn't have a lot of good things to say, what I gathered is that you're an honest doctor. And that's what I need right now."

Ben frowned at this characterization, but he could see that criticism from a less-than-honest man could be construed as a vote of confidence for him.

They arranged to meet in the Food Court. When Ben arrived, Ms. Hunsaker sat at a table in the far corner of the room, away from other people, waiting for him. He guessed she wanted to have a private conversation.

Ben passed the coffee urns—he'd already three cups that morning—and walked directly to the table where she sat with both hands around her coffee cup. He introduced himself, confirmed her identity—she told him to call her Sarah—and sat down. She was probably ten years younger than her brother.

He noticed her hands were bare of rings, which undoubtedly meant her husband wasn't around, either through death or divorce. Her short, dark hair was well-styled, and her blue dress unwrinkled, leading Ben to surmise that she probably changed and got ready before coming to the hospital. He guessed she was staying at Kasner's home while she was in town.

"Thanks for meeting me like this," she said.

"I'm sorry for the circumstances of your visit," Ben said. "How can I help you?"

"The internist or neurologist or whoever is taking care of Herbert said this morning that his brain wave test, whatever you call it—"

"EEG."

She nodded. "Anyway, it showed … well, cutting through the technical jargon … Herbert will never again be a sentient human being. He's being maintained on life support. As his closest blood relative, it will be up to me to allow that support to be discontinued."

Ben frowned. He'd seen something like this coming, but wasn't certain what he could do to help.

"First of all, tell me it's okay to end Herb's life," she said.

Wow. Right to the tough things. "If he'll never function again, you have two choices. He could be confined to either a hospital or—if he lives that long—an extended-care facility. His death would probably come from pneumonia or the consequences of an infection, but he might live for years before that happened."

"And the other choice?" she asked.

"Withdraw life support. The doctor can help you make sure he doesn't suffer during the event."

"Herbert made no provisions for organ donation, but I think it would be the right thing to do. I guess I could ask the nurses, but I'd rather hear about it from a doctor. Do you agree?"

One of the things Ben learned early in his surgical residency was the value of organ donation. "Yes. And the hospital chaplain would be glad to assist you when you decide you want to go that route."

"Do you know his extension by any chance?" Sarah opened her purse and dug into it, eventually pulling out a pen and pad of paper.

"I do." Ben had been down this road before. He thumbed to his contact list on his cell phone. "I think it would be one last thing Dr. Kasner could do for his patients."

Sarah didn't try to hide what she thought of her brother. "Oh, Herb has done some terrible things. And he should have retired a decade ago. This won't make up for some of his mistakes, but I think it will be a start."

The conversation went on for a few more minutes, but it was obvious Sarah had received the answers she needed—or perhaps the assurance—and was ready to move on. She shook hands with Ben, thanked him once more, and left the Food Court.

As Ben stood up to leave, he looked down and saw a tiny ring with two keys—a small one and a longer one—lying on the table. The label said, "Spare office keys." Sarah must have dropped them when she was rummaging in her purse.

Ben looked around and saw that she'd already gone, so

he dropped the ring of keys in his pocket. He could return them later.

Rachel arrived on Two North early Tuesday morning and checked at the desk to see whether Sheila had been transferred to that wing. Sure enough, she found her friend and colleague in a room across from the nurses' station, one arm encased in plaster and elevated on two pillows.

"Looks like you're settled in," Rachel said. "But don't get too comfortable. Your doctor tells me you'll probably be ready to go home tomorrow—maybe even later today."

"And I'm so ready." Sheila rolled her eyes. "Are you sure I haven't thrown too much onto you with this 'acting head nurse' request?"

"I'd never have asked for this, but I'm happy to step in as a favor to you. Now that things have settled down a bit, though, I'm sure nursing service will send someone up here to stand in for you."

"I wouldn't be too sure of that."

Rachel frowned. "What do you mean?"

"I talked with the head of nursing service about my slot. When you get to the desk, you'll find a message to call Jesse Bell. She'll offer you the head nurse's position up here."

"You mean until you return to work."

"Nope." Sheila smiled. "I was going to let you in on this secret yesterday, but my accident and a comminuted fracture of my radius and ulna sort of changed my plans. They took my ring and locked it away yesterday when they were getting me ready for surgery.

Rachel crinkled her forehead. "What ring?"

"Over the weekend, Tom asked me to marry him."

Rachel took Sheila's unaffected hand and squeezed. "Congratulations! I'd give you a big hug, but I'll wait until you're a bit longer post-op."

"And maybe until this cast is off, so there's no danger that I'll club you."

"I didn't know you and Tom were that serious," Rachel said.

"We kept it quiet." Sheila grinned. "But now I guess it's okay to tell everyone."

"I'm so happy for you. But you're coming back to Two North after you're healed, right?"

"Tom has been offered a job in Dallas. He starts in three months. We're getting married—cast and all—and I'm moving with him. That's why they need someone permanent to fill my position, and I've recommended you for the job."

Rachel was shaking her head before Sheila finished talking. "Remember, I've got my own wedding coming up in a few weeks. And Ben and I have decided we can get by on one paycheck if we need to, so I might not continue working."

"I'm sure you'll make the right decision when you think it over. But even if you don't want the job permanently, will you handle the floor until nursing service appoints a new head nurse?"

"Of course." This was the least Rachel could do for her friend. "There are plenty of experienced candidates, so they'll probably fill it soon. Now I need to get to work. And you need to get some rest. But be sure to let me know when Tom comes by. I want to give him a hug." She grinned. "I don't have to be careful with his arm, do I?"

In Rachel's living room that evening, Ben held up a ring

containing two keys—a large brass one and a smaller silver one. "These dropped out of Sarah Hunsaker's purse when I met her. I went by Kasner's ICU room to return them this evening, and she asked me to use them."

"What? Why?"

"She's made the decision to remove Kasner's life support—probably in the morning. Sometime after his death, his office staff will go through his files. Sarah realizes her brother hasn't always done things that would look good in the light of day, and she asked if I'd go through his personal papers and remove anything that others shouldn't see."

Rachel chewed on her lip. "What if you find evidence of something criminal? You can't simply destroy that, can you?"

I'll talk with her after we see what I find," Ben said. "But this is my chance to determine if Kasner had something on people, something he held over their heads."

Rachel frowned. "And you'll be there legally?"

"Absolutely."

"Then I want to go too," she said.

"Why?" Ben asked.

Rachel looked at him and shook her head. "Isn't it obvious? I'll be a witness that you didn't take anything … or plant something."

Later, after a leisurely dinner at one of their favorite restaurants, Ben and Rachel drove to Kasner's office. It was ten o'clock, and the area was deserted. They exited Ben's car and in a few moments, they stood outside the older surgeon's office door. The glass on the door bore the inscription, Herbert Kasner, MD, General Surgery. The large key on the ring allowed them entrance, just as it had opened the locked front door of the building.

When she followed Ben through the door, Rachel encountered a waiting room that was probably twice the size of her fiancé's … with better furniture. Expensive art work hung on the walls.

"I thought you said he didn't have that large a practice," she said.

"I imagine he's been in this office for quite a while, and at one time he probably needed all this room."

A couple of lamps lit the waiting area, providing faint illumination that functioned as security lights. "Shall we turn on the overheads?" Rachel asked.

"No, let's go straight to his office, which should be through that door."

Ben locked the waiting room door behind them and led Rachel past the reception area, where the corridor led to six patient examination rooms, twice what Ben's office provided. After a couple of false starts, they found Kasner's private office, which was locked, but yielded to the same key that opened the front door.

Once inside, Ben flipped on the lights and fingered the small key on the ring. "I see two filing cabinets. One is locked, one isn't. Guess which one has the good stuff."

Ben inserted the key in the locked file cabinet and turned it. The lock popped outward, and all three drawers opened easily. He tried the top one first. "Copies of his medical license, his fellowship in the American College of Surgeons, all his applications and renewals for licensure and narcotics number. That kind of stuff." He closed the drawer. "It won't hurt for the staff to find this."

"What will they do with it?"

"Probably box it all up and send it to Sarah. Whether she keeps it or throws it away will be up to her."

Rachel pointed to the cabinet. "Are you going to open the middle drawer next?"

Ben shook his head. "You know I'm the kind of guy who

eats the crust end of the pie first and leaves the tip for last. I think I'll take the same approach with these files." He pulled out the bottom drawer, thumbed through the manila folders there, then whistled silently. "Rachel, look at this!"

She crouched next to him as he pulled a few folders from the front of the file drawer. They were neatly labelled with the names of the current mayor, a former mayor, and two city councilmen. "What's in them?"

"This one has information about an illegitimate child fathered by one of our upstanding leaders." He dropped that the folder on the floor and opened the next one. "Here's a newspaper story from a town in Nebraska about this guy. He left under a cloud of suspicion to avoid an investigation of his financial dealings on a land purchase."

"It looks like there are at least a dozen folders in the drawer." Rachel eased to the floor, where she sat cross-legged.

Ben looked through the names on the tabs. "Whoa! These files are labeled with the names of four of the more senior doctors in town, as well two members of the hospital board." He pulled another folder out and thumbed through the contents. "This is information about a liaison this doctor had almost twenty years ago. According to these notes, his mistress eventually left town to have an abortion. Never returned."

Rachel peered at the typed sheet in Ben's hand and scanned it before whistling. "This is perfect blackmail material." She pointed to all the files. "He's got something on—"

"On a number of people in key positions. I told you he'd been practicing in this town long enough to know where all the bodies are buried." He nodded toward the files. "I think we've found the graveyard."

"Obviously, this isn't the kind of stuff Kasner's office staff should find," Rachel said. "What do you plan to do with it?"

"I'll talk with Kasner's sister in the morning. She'll have to decide that."

Rachel pointed to the middle file drawer. "If that bottom one has this kind of good stuff, what do you suppose is in here?"

"Let's find out." Ben pulled out the middle file drawer. It was almost empty, containing only four or five folders, none of them fat. He lifted out the one nearest the front. Inside it there were several sheets of lined paper bearing handwritten notes. He passed the folder to Rachel. "What do you make of this?"

"It looks like code of some kind." Each sheet had its own heading. "Doc, Car Guy. I have no idea what any of this means."

He pointed at the top sheet. "Each one lists a bunch of dates and numbers." Ben scanned the page in his hand. "The last entry on this one, the sheet headed 'Car Guy,' has the letter C after the date."

"Do you think that's important?" Rachel handed the sheets of paper back to him.

Ben waved them at her. "I think this could be the key to everything."

"What do you mean?"

"I'm not sure, but I'd guess that we've identified the person who's the head of the drug ring in the region."

"Shouldn't you give this to the police?"

"It's not our decision to make," Ben said. "We entered here at the request of Kasner's next of kin. Theoretically, all this belongs to her, or it will after he's dead—if he isn't already." He straightened up, leaving the file drawer open. "I'll tell her about what we found and advise her to do the right thing."

11

A bit over two weeks after their trip to Kasner's office, Ben and Rachel approached Detective Murchison's desk in the squad room of the Freeman police station. It was Friday afternoon, and things were quiet.

"Your phone call said this was important but not urgent," Ben said to the detective.

"Thanks for coming down," Murchison said. "We're in the process of winding down this investigation, and I think we have some information that might interest you."

"Do you have the person responsible for Rick Hinshaw's murder?" Ben asked.

"Yes. And we've learned the reason behind the death of Miss Gardner's father." Murchison stood. "Why don't you folks come into our interview room where we'll have a little privacy. I'll fill you in on what we've been doing over the past two weeks and the conclusions we've come to." He led the way. "I think you deserve to hear this from me."

When Ben and Rachel were seated in the same interrogation room where they'd been before, Murchison closed the door behind him and took a chair across from them. "Dr. Kasner's sister, Sarah Hunsaker, contacted us and gave us information that allowed us to get a search warrant for his office. As a result of the material we found, plus some investigation afterward, we were able to crack the case." The detective looked directly at Ben. "As I understand it, you went to that office at the request of Ms. Hunsaker. So you know all about what was in the file drawers."

"I advised his sister that she contact the police about the material," Ben said.

"And she agreed," Murchison said. "In one drawer was material Kasner could—I emphasize *could*—have used for blackmail. We quietly notified the people involved and told them how it had come into our possession, and we planned to shred it unless they had other plans." He smiled. "None did."

"What about the rest of it?" Ben asked.

"The folders in one drawer of the file contained the records Kasner kept for all the people working under him distributing narcotics."

"How did you interpret the information in those folders?" Rachel asked. "It looked like it was written in code."

Murchison shoved an acetate envelope containing a photocopy of one of the sheets toward them. "The names at the top of each page are Kasner's designation for the person who heads that particular part of the operation. It wasn't tough to crack the code. We put in some effort over the past couple of weeks, first identifying the people and then gathering evidence against them. Today all of them will be arrested."

"Do we know any of them?" Rachel asked.

"Ms. Gardner, I think you know Car Guy. Joe Durbin has been pushing narcotics for Kasner for two or three years. Matter of fact, he's the one who got your father back on drugs. Since they were readily available to him—Durbin offered them at no charge if your father turned a blind eye to the operation. It didn't take long until your father had that monkey on his back again."

"That means Durbin was the one who supplied that last fatal dose," Ben said.

"It was a special one. See the notation C next to the date? That meant carfentanil, one of the key ingredients in the drug Gray Death. Durbin could have given him uncut heroin, hoping he'd overdose, but instead, he opted for a sure thing. He supplied Mr. Gardner with Gray Death, promising a high like he'd never experienced."

"Why?" Tears swam in Rachel's eyes.

"Durbin wanted to make sure your father wouldn't wake up." The detective paused. "There is essentially no safe dose of Gray Death. Matter of fact, you have to handle it carefully because it can kill some people if they simply contact large amounts of it."

"Why did he want to kill Dad?"

"Durbin was embezzling money from the dealership. At first, he needed cash to buy into Kasner's enterprise, but it was so easy to divert money from the business that he kept stealing, adding the cash to his income. He embezzled over a hundred thousand dollars."

"I still don't understand," Ben said.

"We're pretty certain Mr. Gardner planned to loan him half the money to put back into the company, with some sort of repayment plan for the rest. But Durbin thought there was a better way. He'd collect the key man insurance on your father, replace the money he'd embezzled, and pocket the rest."

"So that's why Dad wanted the money," Rachel said softly.

Murchison raised his eyebrows, inviting Rachel to explain, but Ben held up his hand. "We'll tell you about it later. Meanwhile, would we know anybody else in the drug ring?"

"Yeah … Doc. Rick Hinshaw was about to give us Kasner's name, so he had to be silenced.

"I can't believe it. You mean Rick was involved in dealing drugs?" Ben said.

"No, he was going to blow the whistle. Doc was the guy who shot him." Murchison looked at his watch. "Carl Rosser should be in custody by now."

Later that afternoon, Rachel sat in Miriam Gardner's living room with her arm around her mother. "I know this is hard to hear, but I thought you deserved to learn it from me instead of someone from the police department—or a reporter calling to get your comments."

Miriam wiped her eyes with a tissue from the box on the table. "I guess I have what you'd call mixed feelings. Bill was using drugs again, but at least he didn't take his own life with an overdose. Joe Durbin gave him the stuff that killed him." She stifled a sob. "None of this will bring Bill back, of course."

"But don't forget we learned the real reason Dad was trying to borrow forty-five thousand dollars. It wasn't because he was spending his money on drugs."

"No. Of course, he could have asked me for a loan. I still have the money your grandparents left me, but he'd never do that." Miriam sniffled. "He knew how I felt. I made it clear I didn't want him in my life."

"I guess now you'll run the dealership," Rachel said. "We won't know until the will is filed for probate which of us is Dad's heir, but even if it turns out to be me, I want to pass the dealership on to you.

"But Joe—"

"Joe Durbin is in custody," Rachel said. "I don't know if he'll be charged with distributing drugs or if the district attorney will bring a murder charge against him, but in any case, he's out of the picture."

There were no more tears now. "Do you really want me to run it?"

"If you will."

Her mom's voice took on a confident tone Rachel hadn't heard in a while. "Then I guess I'd better talk with Bill's attorney. We'll see what the legalities are." She reached for her phone. "And I suppose I'd better find out who's running things there now without Joe."

"Will you want my help, Mom?"

"No. I know you wouldn't micro-manage, and I'll certainly ask for your input if it's something important, but I think this is something I should do myself."

Rachel rose and hugged her mother. "And I think you'll do fine." *Dad would be proud.*

In her car, Rachel called Ben's cell phone. Although she was due to see him tonight, she really wanted to talk with him now to tell him about her visit to Carlyle and her mother. His phone rang several times, then rolled over to voicemail. Rachel didn't leave a message.

She thought about it as she drove home. Her name and image would show up as the calling party on Ben's cell phone, so his probable reason for not answering would be that he was busy. Was he on call today? She was certain he wasn't, but things often changed. Perhaps one of the other doctors who was supposed to be taking calls wasn't able to fulfill his duties, and Ben was pressed into service. Or he might be talking with one of his patients. Sometimes the answering service gave him those calls, even when he wasn't on call, knowing that only he could answer the patient's questions.

When Rachel reached the turnoff to her house, she made a snap decision and drove by. She'd go to Ben's apartment. If his car was there, she'd knock on his door. She smiled. It was a beautiful evening, and it looked like the police had wrapped up the problems that had plagued both of them for the past several months. Soon they'd be married and could move forward with their lives.

When she reached Ben's apartment, she found his car in its assigned space. *He's home. I'll surprise him.* Rachel parked in a visitor slot and walked to his apartment. She started to ring the bell, but noticed that the door was ajar a few inches. That was unlike Ben. Had he gone out for some reason and left the door open? No, he was careful to the point of compulsiveness—always securing his doors and windows before leaving, turning off lights behind him, never starting his car until all the passengers had fastened their seat belts.

She put her ear to the crack of the partially open door and heard Ben's voice. "You don't want to do this," he said.

She didn't recognize the other man's voice or hear every word, but she could make out enough to know he was threatening Ben.

Rachel started to use her cell phone to call 9-1-1, but she thought better of it. The appearance of police, even if they approached without lights blazing and sirens sounding, might spook the man. Plus, she wasn't sure Ben had the time before something terrible happened.

Quietly, she opened the door a bit wider and crept inside the entryway. The man's back was toward her, but the way Ben stood with his hands up, she had no doubt he was being held at gunpoint.

Didn't Ben tell her once he had a pistol? "A nice little

five-shot revolver ... safely in the drawer of my entryway table." He told her he didn't want to use it because it was too dangerous to have a gun in his home. Well, now she hoped she intended to make use of it. She slid the drawer open slowly, withdrawing the revolver without making a sound. It felt heavy in her hand.

Ben stood with his hands partially raised, palms outstretched. "You don't want to do this."

"I've been waiting a long time for this day." Carl Rosser aimed a handgun at Ben's chest. *He can't miss at this range. Think, Ben.*

"Every time you acted so high and mighty because you got your surgical training at a famous teaching hospital. The way you took over the ER like you knew more than me." He waved the boxy pistol to emphasize his point. "I was the lowly doc working in the emergency room because I couldn't get the residency I wanted."

Ben stared at the black hole in the barrel of the gun, his mind going a mile a minute. "Carl, be reasonable." Ben forced himself to remain calm. "I didn't—"

"Of course, you couldn't know that I had a much more profitable source of income than the pittance I got for working in the ER. And that money would have kept rolling in until you and that nurse stuck your noses in."

"We're not responsible for—"

"Shut up! Kasner figured you were trouble from the get-go. That's why he tried to discourage you. I guess he thought if he caused you enough trouble, you'd close your practice and start fresh in another town. . But you were too stubborn or too stupid. Either way, it ends right now."

"Carl, we can—"

"You think I care what you have to say?" He laughed. "I saw the police when they came to arrest me. I realized what was going on, so I ducked out the back way. I could have left town right away, but I swore I'd get revenge on you before I left."

Ben had watched Rachel from the moment she tip-toed inside on stocking-clad feet. Now she held the pistol he kept in his drawer. Would she use it? In the meantime, he couldn't let Carl know she was behind him. The madman wouldn't hesitate to kill her too. "Carl, put the gun down. We can work this out."

"There's nothing to work out. I'll shoot you. Then I'll stop by your girlfriend's house and take care of her. After that—"

Ben's heart almost stopped as he watched Rachel cover the last few feet to where Rosser stood. Part of him wanted to shout for her to run, but if he opened his mouth, she could be shot before she made it out of the door. And part of him was hoping for what happened next.

"The hard thing you feel in your back is the barrel of a revolver," Rachel said in a strong voice. "My finger is on the trigger, and I'd like nothing better than to pull it."

Rosser stood frozen.

Rachel's voice never wavered. "My first shot will sever your spinal cord, leaving you paralyzed from the waist down. If I have to shoot again, it will be into the base of your skull." She paused, apparently pushing the pistol barrel a bit harder to emphasize her point. "Now drop your gun. Then get down on your knees, with your hands behind your head. Now!"

Despite the look of hate that flashed in Rosser's eyes, he did as he was told. Once the doctor dropped to his knees, Ben picked up the semiautomatic pistol Rosser had let slide out of his hand and aimed it at the intruder's head. Without turning, he said to Rachel, "I guess I owe you my life."

She was breathing heavily, almost to the point of hyperventilation. "I … I'm glad I remembered your talking about this pistol in the drawer of your entryway table."

Ben managed a slight head shake. "If we keep it around I need to take you to the range and teach you a bit more about that gun."

"What … what do you mean?"

"You were great when you stuck the barrel in Rosser's back. And you convinced me you were ready to pull the trigger." He nodded at the revolver in Rachel's hand. "That gun doesn't have a safety. It's a double-action pistol, and it takes a strong pull on the trigger to fire it, especially if you don't cock it by pulling back the hammer."

"Believe me," she said. "With the barrel right up against him, I was ready to pull the trigger as hard as necessary." Rachel lowered the weapon. "But I'm glad I didn't have to."

Tomorrow would mark a month since the police wrapped up the case that had cost Rick Hinshaw and Bill Gardner their lives. After Dr. Herb Kasner's death, his sister had arranged for his cremation and taken his ashes to Kansas where she buried them in the family plot. Carl Rosser was behind bars, awaiting trial for drug distribution and attempted murder. Joe Durbin was also in custody, charged with murder. Miriam Gardner was running the dealership her ex-husband Bill had left behind and doing it well.

Life for Rachel Gardner and Ben Merrick had settled down. It wasn't normal yet, but it was getting there. With the understanding that she would be getting married in a few weeks, Rachel accepted the temporary assignment of head nurse on Two North at Freeman Memorial Hospital. Despite her duties, she still found time to see Ben every day, although their time together was shorter than she wished. Their plans for a wedding hadn't changed—a small ceremony at the church, maybe a long weekend for a honeymoon, and then back to work.

When it became clear there was no encumbrance to the insurance company paying off Bill Gardner's insurance, Rachel offered to share the proceeds with her mom, but her mother refused. "I have my own money. And besides, I now have the income from the dealership, and that will be bolstered by the key man insurance your father left behind. Use the proceeds from your dad's policy for you and Ben."

And that's what Rachel intended to do. It was time to have a serious conversation with Ben, one she'd been delaying for several days. That's why Ben rode in the passenger seat in her car on this bright, sunny Saturday afternoon. Rachel hoped and prayed Ben would agree to accept her surprise.

Ben had argued at first about her driving, until she said, "There's a reason. Trust me."

He looked out the window at the passing scenery. "This is a nice part of town. You know, I've been in Freeman for a couple of years, but I don't think I've ever driven through this area before."

"That's because this is a nicer neighborhood than the one where you and I live. Like most young doctors and nurses, especially the single ones, we've stuck close to the hospital where we work. We live near it. We go to restaurants or order takeout from places near there. We even choose cleaners and grocery stores in that area."

She turned right and brought the car to a halt at the end of the cul-de-sac in front of a two-story house with a large yard. There was no car in the driveway and no sign of activity evident inside the house.

Rachel turned off the car's ignition. She turned and smiled at Ben. "Like it?"

Ben looked out the window, then turned to face Rachel. "From the outside, it looks great. Someone has done a good job on the yard. I don't know about inside, but I imagine it's nice as well. But why are we looking here? I thought we planned to move into your house after the wedding."

"That's what I want to talk with you about."

Seeing Ben's puzzled expression, she hurried to explain. "After Mother declined any part of the proceeds from Dad's insurance policy, I found this house and put down a deposit to hold it. If you don't like it, all I'll lose is the earnest money. But if you like it, I can make a substantial down payment from the proceeds of my father's insurance policy. After that, we can afford the payments on my salary alone, much less our combined incomes."

"So …"

Rachel produced a key from the pocket of her jeans. "The house is ours if you want it. I've already looked at it, and it's wonderful from my standpoint. Now I need your approval."

"But our plans—"

"We can change those plans. I've checked with a realtor, and she thinks there'll be no problem selling my house. The lease on your apartment expires right after our wedding." Rachel looked at Ben's face. "I know Dad did some bad things, but I think he'd be pleased if we use the proceeds of his insurance to start our married life in this home. What do you say?"

Ben took a moment before he replied. "You mean, would I think about all the bad things he did each time I walked through the door of this house?"

Rachel nodded.

"No. I'd think that Bill Gardner left behind something that allowed us to get a good start on our new life together. How about you?"

Rachel leaned over and kissed him. "Me, too. Would you like to look at the inside?"

Ben opened the car door. "If you like it, I'm sure I will. Let's take a tour of our new home."

Rachel slid out from under the steering wheel, joined hands with her fiancé, and walked toward the home where they'd start their new life. *Thank you, Dad.*

HERE'S A PREVIEW OF
DR. MABRY'S NEXT NOVEL,
GUARDED PROGNOSIS

"I didn't get much sleep last night, so I'm afraid I'll be slower this morning." Dr. James Taggart stifled a yawn. "What does the schedule look like?" He sipped coffee and leaned on the front desk at his office, while his nurse/receptionist, Martha, looked at the appointment book.

"It looks like you have a little time," Martha said. "Our first patient cancelled, so there's half an hour before the next one's due."

"Good." He swept a lock of black hair out of his eyes, then rubbed them as he yawned.

"I'm sorry you lost that patient the other day," she said. "But I guess when a chain-saw cuts that deep into the leg …"

"Yeah, it got the femoral artery, and I couldn't stop the bleeding." He shook his head. "Not a very good way to build a practice. Especially since at least one member of the man's family is saying that he died because of my incompetence."

"Do you think they'll sue?"

"I don't know what they'll do," James said. *Actually, I think I know what one of them is doing, and I hope it stops soon.* "I imagine the family will cool off, but I know how I'd feel if my father died like that."

"Speaking of your father," Martha said. "He called just before you came in. Said it wasn't urgent, and that you'd know the number."

James figured that when his father took time from his own surgical practice to call, the urgency was implied. He started to mention this to Martha, but decided she had no way of knowing his father's idiosyncrasies. In the two years she'd worked for James, he might have mentioned his dad half a dozen times. And so far as he could recall, this was the first time Henry Taggart had phoned James at the office. "I'll call him now," he said, and turned away.

He didn't so much sit down at his desk in a normal fashion as collapse into the swivel chair behind it, pulling the phone toward him in the same motion. He stifled a yawn as he reached to dial. His father had told Martha that James knew his dad's office number. Actually, he had to search his memory for it. True, he'd called his father before … but not recently. Not at the office, not at home. Not since—

"Dr. Taggart's office."

"Jean," he said, "This is James Taggart. My dad called me. Is he with a patient?"

"He's just finishing. Can you hang on for a minute? I know he wants to talk with you."

There was nothing particularly unusual in Jean's words, but James heard an undertone, some emotion not expressed. He couldn't tell what it was, but it set off his radar. Concern, perhaps? First his father called, a rarity in itself. Then, when James returned the call, Jean sounded … what? Worried? James had a bad feeling.

It wasn't long before Dr. Henry Taggart picked up the phone. "James. Thanks for calling back."

James started with the question foremost in the mind of most children when a parent phones them. "Dad, is everything okay?" he said. "Has something happened to you or mom?"

"So far as I know, your mother is fine. I visited the nursing home this past weekend. The staff is taking good care of her, and her doctor checks on her periodically." He paused. "I'm afraid I'm the one who has a little problem."

The sinking feeling James experienced was like the one he got in a glass elevator that went down too rapidly. "For you to admit you have a problem—even a 'little one'—worries me. What is it?"

"I've been having some vague digestive symptoms," the elder Taggart said. "It went on long enough that I finally checked with my internist. He poked and prodded, then persuaded me to have a GI series. After I—"

Despite the air conditioning in his office, James felt a trickle of sweat running between his shoulder blades. "Dad, skip the details of the workup. Just tell me what Dr. Geist found."

Apparently, Henry Taggart wasn't about to be hurried. "After the initial X-rays, he and I talked. He wants me to see a specialist, but thinks it may be something really bad."

"What is it?" James almost shouted into the phone. One diagnosis shoved all the others out of his mind. *Please, God, not that one.*

"He thinks it's most likely pancreatic carcinoma."

James felt acid in the back of his throat pushing to get out. His pulse was like a windstorm in his ears. Was that right?

Pancreatic carcinoma. To a surgeon like James, this translated into a virtual death sentence. The diagnosis was almost never made in time to do anything more than give palliative or experimental treatment. The son in him wanted to drop everything and rush home. The physician, on the other hand, began to think through the various treatment options and the places they could be administered.

"Hold on, there. I know what you're thinking," his father continued. "Fred wants me to see the oncologists at the university medical center. They've got a good team of specialists over there, and I'm sure they're ready to jump in when—or more accurately, if— I let them. I just wanted to let you know what's going on."

"Dad, why do you say 'if? Aren't you planning to let the doctors handle this?"

"Probably," Henry said. "But we both know that if this is pancreatic cancer, the outlook is pretty grim."

"Dad—"

Before James could respond further, his father added, "And I may need your help."

"You mean you want me to take over treatment?" James asked.

"No. I may need you to assist me if I decide to commit suicide."

Books by Richard L. Mabry, MD

Novels of Medical Suspense
Code Blue
Medical Error
Diagnosis Death
Lethal Remedy
Stress Test
Heart Failure
Critical Condition
Fatal Trauma
Miracle Drug
Medical Judgment
Cardiac Event

Novellas
Rx Murder
Silent Night, Deadly Night
Doctor's Dilemma
Surgeon's Choice

Non-Fiction
The Tender Scar: Life After the Death of A Spouse

WHAT OTHERS SAY ABOUT RICHARD MABRY'S BOOKS

About *Medical Judgment*: "Balances action with emotion and struggles of faith, making it easy for readers to care about the characters and what happens to them in all the twists and turns of the genre."

Lauraine Snelling, best-selling author of the Red River of the North sagas

About *Miracle Drug*: "Excellent story. Excellently crafted. Great characters. Great plot."

DiAnne Mills, Christy-award winning author of *Deadlock*

About *Fatal Trauma*: "Asks big questions of faith, priorities, and meaning, all within the context of a tightly crafted medical drama."

Steven James, best-selling author of *Placebo* and *Checkmate*

About *Critical Condition*: "Has the uncommon ability to take medical details and make them understandable, while still maintaining accuracy and intrigue."

Romantic Times Book Reviews (4 ½ stars)

About *Heart Failure*: "Combines his medical expertise with a story that will keep you on the edge of your seat."
USA Today

About *Stress Test*: "Original and profound. I found the ... story (moving) a mile a minute."
Michael Palmer, *NYT* best-selling author of *Oath of Office*

About *Lethal Remedy*: "His thrillers balance thrills with the great heart and loving relationships that make us most human."
The Big Thrill (International Thriller Writers)

About *Diagnosis Death*: "Full of sudden twists and turns, the novel's fast pace makes it hard to put down."
Romantic Times Book Reviews (4 ½ stars).

About *Medical Error*: "Kept me guessing as I eagerly turned the pages."
Angela Hunt, author of *When Darkness Comes*

About *Code Blue*: "Rarely does a debut novel draw me in and rivet my attention as (this one) did."
B. J. Hoff, author of The Emerald Ballad Series

38348375R00071

Made in the USA
Middletown, DE
07 March 2019